BOOK 5
THE PEAKS SAGA

The FOUNTAIN and the DESERT

M.F. ERLER

THE FOUNTAIN AND THE DESERT, Book 5
by M.F. Erler

Published by

WESTWIND PRESS
an imprint of First Steps Publishing
PO Box 571
Gleneden Beach, Oregon 97388-0571
FirstStepsPublishing.com

ISBN: 978-1-937333-97-3 (hb)
978-1-937333-83-6 (pb)
978-1-937333-98-0 (epub)

Cover illustration by Kabita Studios
Cover design, interior formatting by Suzanne Fyhrie Parrott

Please provide feedback

10 9 8 7 6 5 4 3 2

Printed in U.S.A.

Praise for the Peaks Saga...

"I remember fondly reading The Lion, The Witch, and The Wardrobe *when I was in middle school.* The Peaks at the Edge of the World *has a similar mix of fantasy and adventure with a moral tale at its center. This is a book that's appropriate for a younger audience than most sci fi/fantasy novels. Enjoy the read!"*

—Kathy Dunnehoff
ZOLA AWARD-WINNING WOMEN'S FICTION WRITER

"...a page turner!" *—Judith Seidel*

"Ms. Erler puts religion in new settings as she uses the characters in both the past and the future to meld the consequences of a religion lost, then found, then challenged. The ride is exciting. The characters real and engaging."

—Charlene Hecht
BA MUSIC EDUCATION
LONGTIME WRITER, INCLUDING "GUNSMOKE" FAN FICTION

"M.F. Erler skillfully pioneers a new writing genre, mixing elements of science fiction, dimensional time-travel, and modern Christian spirituality. She uses likeable characters in well-crafted settings in which we can identify with their real-life struggles."

—Richard Bartlett, MA, PhD

"...[M.F.] Erler's book, with its futuristic sci-fi focus and true-to-life grittiness, is not your typical Christian novel. At times, it unabashedly describes the realities of the darkness of humanity in order to contrast it with the power of hope and love found in God's grace. This unique book is well worth your time to read and I highly recommend it."

—Pastor Kevin Bueltmann
TRINITY LUTHERAN CHURCH - ASSOCIATE PASTOR
TRINITY LUTHERAN CAMP - EXECUTIVE DIRECTOR

Books by M.F. Erler
THE PEAKS SAGA

This book is dedicated to My Brother, Dan
who has a great imagination, too.

Contents

"Answer me quickly, O Lord, for my spirit fails. Do not hide your face from me or I will go down to the pit. Let the morning bring me word of your unfailing love, for I have put my trust in you. Show me the way I should go, for to you I lift up my soul."

— *Psalm 143:7-8*

ACKNOWLEDGMENTS

Thanks to all my readers, and especially –

Richard, who has been a faithful beta reader for me, and who has given me much emotional support.

Emilie, who is more than a daughter, also a friend, who reminds me to think positively.

Nancy, an old friendship being renewed, who is reminding me of the value of life and faith.

Margie, a new friendship developing, with someone I trust as a sister in the faith.

Pastor Greg, whose music still speaks to me, even after all these years. I appreciate your letting me use the lyrics, PG.

FOREWORD
SUMMER FLIGHT

It only happened once –
      In a warm summer,
   A new place where I'd always dreamed of being:
      With sky and stars
      Mountains and trees
   And that glowing person
        — the embodiment of all my dreams.

And so, with wings of clouds
     And sparkling sun on water,
I took flight toward heaven -
    and the fulfillment of my girlish dreams.

But all this faded and disappeared –
       as grey clouds of flatland closed in.
   Never has it come again.

Perhaps that childish, dream-colored,
      dancing part of me
   just continued its flight on
      above the mornings and the mountains—
For the rest of me wonders where it went.

                        MFE, 1971

The Sullien Family Tree

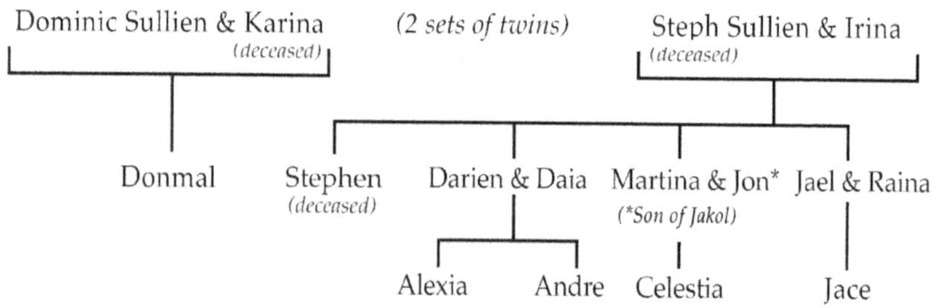

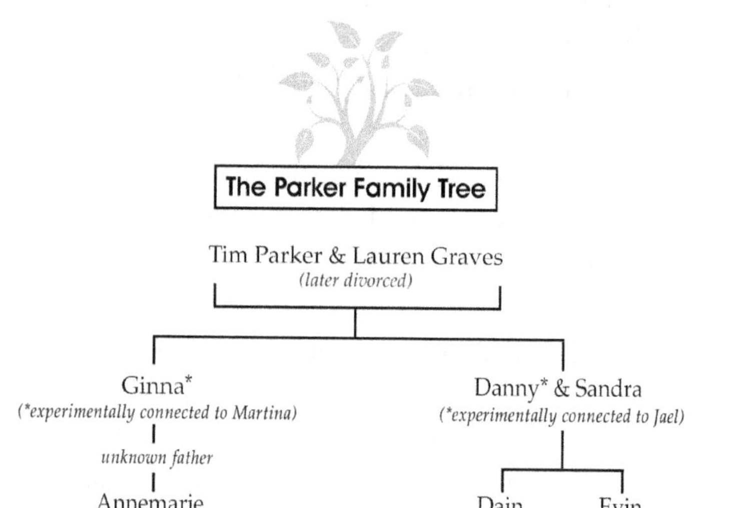

The Parker Family Tree

PROLOGUE
DUST IN THE WIND

From *"Searching for Maia"*

Danny Parker sighed and began tracing patterns in the dust on the windowsill. He felt a lump rising in his throat and tried desperately to swallow it. 'I'm too old to cry!' he told himself. 'I'm almost fourteen years old. I have to be the man of this house now that Dad is gone for good.'

Despite his efforts, tears were already trickling down his cheeks. Two of them dropped into the dust on the sill and spread into strange patterns. Looking down through tear-blurred eyes, he blinked at the picture he saw. His finger had drawn a jagged line like a range of mountains. The tear shapes looked like two figures walking toward him out of a haze.

Yes, that really happened once, though it was over four years ago now, and seemed like forever. Jon and Jael came to them out of time—what they called the GAP. Jael shared the story of his life, and they found hope and strength to face their trials in this new home. But now that seemed so long ago. The hope he and Ginna once felt seemed to have dried up and blown away, with the dust in the wind out here on the barren plains.

Suddenly a terribly strong gust shook the house. Afraid the window might blow in, Danny stepped back, covering his face with his arm. When he looked at the window again, two blond figures were standing there, gazing into his eyes.

"Ginna!" he cried. "They're back! The time-travelers who took us across the Galactic Antipaterminal Passage."

His sister poked her head out her bedroom door. "Who's back?" she demanded. "What are you bugging me for?"

"Jon and Jael are here," he said, trying to keep his voice from wavering.

The two figures smiled at him and stepped aside to reveal a third figure standing just behind them. This one was a girl only slightly taller than Jael. Her dark brown hair hung long and straight to her shoulders, and her deep green eyes seemed to flash as she glanced over at Ginna, who'd just stepped out of her door.

"I'm Martina Sullien, Jael's sister," she said. "We came at your call, Daniel and Virginia."

"Don't call me that! My name is Ginna! And what did you have to call *them* for, anyway? Do we need another lecture on hope and faith?"

Danny flinched noticeably at her words. "I'm sorry," he said to the three standing before him. "She's just not herself lately."

"Maybe I'm finally learning to *be* myself for a change," said Ginna, stepping closer to them now.

"Perhaps you are, Ginna," came Martina's voice, very calm and even. "I know how difficult that can be, believe me."

Something in her manner seemed to calm Ginna. "I'm sorry," she murmured. "It's so strange to see Jon and Jael here. I'd almost decided it was all just a dream. It seems so long ago now." Her voice tapered into a wistful tone.

"Time is a very relative thing," said Jon. "Who can say what time has done in its many flowing directions since last we talked?"

"*I* can see that Daniel is taller," Jael said. "He's almost as tall as I am."

"So he is," Jon agreed. "Now, why have you *both* called us this time?"

"You mean I called, too?" Ginna asked incredulously.

"It appears so since Martina is here," said Jon.

"Well, I think you can guess why I called," said Danny, glancing at Ginna out of the corner of his eye. "We just don't seem to be communicating the way we used to. Something has come between us."

"Or perhaps something is missing between you," said Martina softly.

"Well, I guess it could be that," Ginna muttered. She was standing next to Danny now, her eyes still fixed on Martina. "Why do I feel I know you already?" she asked at last.

"Our lives may have touched before without our knowing it," Martina replied.

"But how?"

"Is she a forerunner, too?" Danny asked.

"Not exactly," Jon replied. "It's more complicated than that. When we were here before, we told you we were from the future because it was the simplest explanation. But that isn't completely accurate. Let me try another way. Have you heard of parallel universes?"

"No," said Danny.

"I have," Ginna said. "In physics class. Worlds that are sort of next to ours, but we can't see them. One is positive, and the other negative."

"Some are opposites like that, but not all," Jon smiled. He turned to the blinds on the window beside them. "Here's a simple way to explain it. These blinds are colored on one side, white on the other, right?" He closed the shades.

They both nodded.

"This blue side represents *your* world," he said. "You see only this side. If we were on the other side, we'd see only our world, just the white side."

"I get it!" cried Danny. "When they're opened just

the right amount, we can see both sides at once—both worlds."

"That's right, Daniel."

"So when we see you, our worlds are touching," mused Ginna, "The blinds are open."

"Not only when you *see* us," said Martina. "Sometimes you sense us in other ways than sight."

"And sometimes you can just feel our presence subconsciously without realizing it," Jael added.

"But I sure haven't felt you lately," said Danny. "It's been really lonely around here."

Ginna glared at him. "Well, it's not all *my* fault."

"Wait," said Jon quietly. "We've come to help as much as we can."

"Are you going to tell us more of your story, Jael?" asked Danny.

"Jon is the story-teller this time," said Jael.

"Yes, now you'll get to see my point of view," Jon nodded. "But I'm not going to just tell you this time. I'm going to take you with me through the blinds to my world. That is, if you're willing to come."

"But how?" Ginna demanded.

"As Jael and Martina," he said softly.

"You mean in their bodies? That's impossible!" she cried.

"I love that word impossible," Jon smiled. "Haven't you read, 'With God, all things are possible'?"

"But I don't want to be lost in someone else's body," she said. "What if we can't come back?"

"It's all right, Ginna," said Danny suddenly, looking into Jael's eyes. "Jael and I have touched many times before, I think. At times, we're almost the same person."

"Remember, we live in parallel worlds," Jon added. "This wouldn't work, otherwise."

"You mean in our world I'm Ginna, but in yours I'm Martina?"

"That's one way to explain it," the tall blond nodded.

"Then right now, am I talking to myself? Looking at myself?"

"Is this any different from looking at yourself in a mirror or talking to yourself when you're alone?"

"Well, I guess it's not. But I'm still afraid," Ginna finally admitted.

Martina stepped forward, taking her hand. "We're all a little afraid of ourselves sometimes, afraid of what we'll find hidden in the deepest recesses of our minds. But it's much better to face those fears and let them flow past us. Then we can learn and move on."

Now Jael stepped forward and took Danny's hand. "Will you do it?" he asked.

"Yes," Danny nodded.

Ginna gave a wordless nod, too.

"Everyone join hands in a GAP circle," Jon said. "And close your eyes."

Even with their eyes closed, they saw a honey-colored light begin to glow in the center of the circle, its warmth radiating toward them, then flowing through them. One moment, Danny was standing between Jael and Martina, with Ginna between Martina and Jon. Then Jael seemed to be gone. Danny found himself holding a larger, stronger hand. It could only be Jon's.

The honey-colored light filled the room now. Someone looking in through the open blinds would have seen three figures standing in a circle, bathed in the rich light. Then the light seemed to flow out of the window, through the blinds, and the figures were gone.

Many GAP-crossings later, another dark-haired woman was standing next to Ginna, reaching for her hand. She knew this was Martina's daughter.

"Are you sure you have the right coordinates for the Fountain, Celestia?" she asked.

"Yes, these are straight from my father, Jon. Remember Ginna? He took you there when you were 'within' my mother."

Ginna looked sidewise at her daughter Annemarie. And then her gaze drifted to the tall gray-haired man who they believed was her father. She saw Garek blush and look down at the ground beneath their feet. Yes, it was still difficult to wrap her mind around all the mysteries surrounding her daughter—and what had happened when she was 'within' Martina.

"All right," Celestia's voice cut into her thoughts. "If you three really want to find the True Fountain, we need to go now. Join hands in a GAP-circle."

As Ginna took Celestia's hand, Garek pressed his hand into hers. It felt so strong and warm. Then she looked across the circle at her daughter and realized Annemarie was standing between both her parents, at last

CHAPTER 1
QUESTIONS

The last thing I remembered was standing in the GAP (Galactic Antipaterminal Passage) circle across from Celestia, our guide. Being first-born like her, I felt the sensation of the earth disappearing beneath my feet, as though it had just fallen away.

Like other crossings I'd been on with her, I expected the ground of our destination—far across the continent—to come up and meet my soles. But it didn't. 'Something must have gone wrong.' I said to myself.

Instead, I was floating in a dense white fog, sensing nothing, not even heat or cold, for what seemed a long time. Then, bit by bit, I regained the feeling of hands holding mine. One I knew was my mother, Ginna Parker. I made out her short brown hair. Her hands had a familiar, comfortable feel, too. My other hand was being clutched by a larger, stronger hand. A man's?

Yes, now I remembered. It was Garek Carson, who Mom claimed was my long-unknown father. If this was true, my blond hair came from him, though his hair showed streaks of gray.

Gradually, the fog began to clear, and I could make out the faces of the three people in this circle with me. My feet finally felt some ground, but it was rocky and hot—not at all like the forest we'd left when we started our journey in the GAP—cutting across the dimensions of space and time. By now, my heart was thumping hard in my chest, and I pulled my hands free from those holding mine.

Ignoring the others, I stared at dark-haired Celestia. I needed answers.

CHAPTER 2
ANNEMARIE'S CLEFT IN THE ROCK

"Where are we? What are we supposed to do now? Mom? Celestia?" I wanted to grab someone and shake an answer out of them as the fear flowed through me.

"I wish I could tell you all exactly where we are, but I'm not sure, Annemarie," sighed Celestia. As she shook her head, her long, dark hair swung at her shoulders.

My mother was nodding. "It appears we're in a desert. Wasn't that where we were heading?"

"Yes, we're trying to find the Rebel Outpost near the Fountain in the Desert. My father said we'd get some help in finding the True Fountain here," Celestia added.

"But is this the right place?" The deeper voice of a man seemed strange to my ears as Garek spoke.

Now I remembered. We were hoping to find the Fountain in the Desert. Celestia's parents had traveled there when she was a baby. They said it washed away all their mistakes, and they even saw a glimpse of Paradise.

"But no one is anywhere in sight," sighed Mom.

"And it's so sweltering hot," I moaned. My long hair was sticking to my neck.

Just as I said this, Garek sank to the ground. As I moved closer to him, I saw how pale his face was and hoped he wasn't having a heat stroke.

Celestia joined me in kneeling beside him. "Are you all right, Garek?"

He chuckled a bit. "I'm just not used to this time travel stuff, I guess. I've only done it a couple of times, you know."

"That's right," Celestia nodded. "But this wasn't supposed to be a Time-GAP. We were only trying to cross the distance from my parents' cave to the Fountain as fast as possible. A typical trip would have taken several weeks."

"Not to mention the dangers of System Patrols," he added. "I remember now what happened when they attacked the Safe Zone."

"Yes, that battle sent all the Rebels scattering to the four winds. I'm not sure where anyone is now," sighed Celestia. "I just hope my parents are still safe in their cave."

"I'm sure they're okay," I patted her arm, noticing how hot it was.

She nodded. "Yes, Annemarie, I'm praying for them."

I couldn't think of a reply to this. Praying was something I hadn't done much lately. When I looked up toward Mom, I noticed how her eyes were focused away from Garek. There was a tension between them I didn't understand. 'Why is she avoiding contact with him whenever she can?' I said to myself. 'After all, she seemed relieved when we traveled to Celestia's time and found him. She spent many long nights nursing him back to health after the battle. Why is she drawing away from him now? I know he cares for her, but she seems afraid of getting emotionally involved with him. Or perhaps with anyone.'

Guilt washed through me. 'Is her hesitation related to how I tested her—running off, blaming her for problems in my life that weren't her fault?'

As these thoughts were filtering through my mind, I was gazing at our present surroundings. Above us loomed a tall red sandstone cliff. A few scrubby pinyons and junipers clustered in the more-shaded areas at the cliff's base. 'Shaded' was only a relative term, though, for the desert sun seemed to beat down on us everywhere, trying to drain our strength as quickly as it could. Still, the bit of shelter beneath these scrubby trees was better than none.

"If there is an outpost here, it's certainly well-hidden," Mom shrugged.

Celestia nodded. "Why didn't I think of that? Of course, they'd keep out of sight until they knew we weren't enemies."

"But how do we go about finding them, if they *are* well-hidden?" I asked. "Wasn't there some way your mother had of focusing on certain people while she crossed the GAP?"

Celestia nodded. "That's not an ability of first-borns, though."

"And I take it we're all first-born, aren't we?" Garek muttered.

"I wish my dad had given me more details about looking for Rebel out-claves and outposts," sighed Celestia.

"Hey, it's not your fault—or his." He smiled at the two of us, and I felt the warmth he relayed through his pale blue eyes.

I was almost embarrassed at his familiarity, though I couldn't say why. Perhaps this was what Mom was feeling, too. 'Maybe that's why she's holding back right now,' I thought. 'Because she believes he really *is* my father, and she's not sure how to face him. She keeps talking about how I have his eyes. Maybe I do. But there's no mirror around, so I have to take her word for it.'

Of course, I knew all the signs did point to Garek being my dad, and I was mostly glad we'd found him—despite all the problems it had caused for the others.

"So, what do you suggest we do next?" Mom's pointed question snapped my mind back to our present reality.

"It seems to me we should try to rest here in what shade we can find until the heat drops at sunset." I was grateful to Garek for jumping in with this suggestion.

"He's right. We can't do any traveling in this heat," Celestia agreed.

"I remember how we traveled only by night on the first trip to the True Fountain," Mom added.

"You remember?" Celestia and Garek said together.

"Yes, I was 'inside' Martina then—or have you forgotten?"

They both nodded and looked down, embarrassed, apparently not wanting to face the facts of how I'd come to be. It all went back to a seemingly innocent affair Garek had with Celestia's mother, Martina, when they were working together on a Forestry Commission Project in the city of Salien.

This was during the time my mother, Ginna, was living 'within' Martina, as part of a parallel universe experiment. According to Celestia's father, Jon, they were two sides of the same person, each living in their world, but they could be merged. The unexpected result of this experiment was my conception. Celestia wasn't Garek's child because she had her father's brown eyes, not Garek's bright blue—which I had.

"If we don't find some Rebels to help us soon, we're going to be in big trouble," Celestia sighed. "We don't have enough food or water to last more than a day or two."

Suddenly Mom seemed to gather her courage. She stepped up to Celestia and took her hand. "Try not to waste energy worrying," she smiled. "Somehow the Lord will help us—after all, he has so far, hasn't he?"

Looking up into Mom's pale brown eyes, I felt my heart lift a little. "Thanks for reminding me, Ginna," Celestia nodded. "Why don't we pray?"

I could see Mom's face light up when Celestia said this. By this time, she'd pulled all four of us into a circle of hands, but I was thinking to myself, 'Will this do any good? The Lord never seems to hear my prayers.'

"Dear Lord," came Celestia's quiet voice, "We don't know where we are, or what we should do. But *you* know, and so we ask you to help us see what we need to do next."

"We're not asking for any vision of the whole picture," Mom added. "Just help us to trust in you, one step at a time."

I felt Garek squeeze my left hand and passed this on to Mom, who was on my right. It made me feel good that he was beginning to understand a little about faith. After all, this was what brought us out here looking for the Fountain in the first place. I knew I needed to find faith as much as he did.

"Thank you," Celestia sighed then. I looked up and saw her smiling at all of us. Apparently, the reassuring hand-squeeze made its way around the circle to her. I could tell by the way Garek was glancing at her that she'd passed it back to him.

"I think we say 'amen' now, don't we?" he smiled. The white orb of the hot sun was still bearing down on us. "Let's try to find a cooler spot to rest," he suggested, getting slowly to his feet.

Just then there came a roaring sound from the air above us. Panic seized me as I remembered the machine-bird mutant Robo-raptors we encountered when we first came to Celestia's time. Without even thinking, I dropped flat on the ground.

"What is it?" Garek's voice shouted.

"Is it a Robo-raptor?" cried Mom.

"Sure looks like a strange one," came Celestia's voice.

Now that I thought of it, there was something different about this sound. Gingerly, I pushed myself up just enough to look toward the sky. Shading my eyes, I stared in surprise and disbelief.

"It looks more like a vehicle from the late Twentieth Century," I said, above the roar. "Like a helicopter."

"A what?" asked Celestia.

"Helicopter," I shouted again. "You've never seen one?"

Celestia was shaking her head. "Is it dangerous?"

"Depends on who's the pilot, I guess. My advice is to get to the ridge as fast as we can."

"Right," Celestia nodded. "Are you up to it, Garek?"

"Let's go for it," he nodded.

"Are you sure you're strong enough to move again?" I asked. After all, he'd nearly fainted just a little while ago.

"I'm feeling much better." He smiled and stood without help.

As quickly as possible, we moved out of the scrub and across the desert again, toward the rocky ridge. I couldn't help glancing nervously overhead, wondering where that helicopter had come from, and where had it gone?

We reached the base of the rock wall and gingerly began walking along a slight path on its edge.

Soon, I heard the soft melody of a bird calling. When we stopped to listen for its song again, there came another most welcome sound.

"Is that water?"

"Sure sounds like it, Mom," I said with excitement.

"Hopefully it's not our imaginations," added Garek.

We stopped talking so we could follow the sounds. The bird's quiet song came again, this time closer. I began moving my hands along the sheer rock wall above us. It was searing hot from the sun, but then I detected the tiniest wet spot. Running my hands up slowly, I found a damp trickle to my right. We all moved closer and saw a shaded crack previously hidden from sight.

As I stepped nearer, it seemed to open out just wide enough for me to slide into, if I turned sideways. By the time I'd worked my way in, the others were close behind me.

"Is this the Fountain?" Garek whispered, his voice full of awe.

"It doesn't look right to me," replied Mom.

I realized with a start that she was the only one of us who'd ever been to the Fountain.

"I think it's just a spring," Celestia nodded to her. "But we surely need the water."

Garek was already dipping his hand into a tiny puddle collected in an indentation in the rock. "It's nice and cool," he smiled, splashing some onto his face.

"Do you think it's safe to drink?" Mom asked.

"I'm not going to worry about that," he chuckled. "Anything beats dying of thirst."

Each of us took a sip from the tiny pool in the red rock, and every time one of us dipped a handful of water, the pool seemed to refill itself from nowhere.

"This place reminds me of an old song," Mom whispered. "I think Eli sang it to us at the Fountain when he took us there." Soon she was singing softly:

'He hideth my soul in the cleft of the rock,
That shadows a dry, thirsty land,
He hideth my soul in the depths of his love,
And covers me there with his hand...'

"I remember hearing that song when I was little, Mom. And I remember part of another one." I began to sing:

'Rock of Ages, cleft for me.
Let me hide myself in thee...'

"I've heard that one at some of our Gatherings," Celestia said in surprise. "It must be a very old song."

"Yes," Mom nodded. "It was already over a century old in my time."

"That's amazing," said Garek.

"I find it reassuring how Believers still express the same faith in songs that my generation did—and the generations before mine." I could hear the awe in Mom's voice and saw her smile and close her eyes. 'Perhaps she's giving thanks to the Lord,' I thought. 'I sure wish I could be like her.'

Garek, meanwhile, pushed back some of the low-hanging greenery just beyond the tiny pool of water. "Look, there's probably enough room for all of us to lie down."

"And it *is* much cooler in here," nodded Mom.

"Wow, Mom, just like your song—a hiding place in the cleft of the rock."

"These shrubs look like tamarisks," Celestia said as she crawled through them.

"They're not as prickly as the junipers and pinyons, either," added Garek, with a smile.

All of us found a spot to stretch out under the low-hanging branches of the tamarisks. In what seemed no time at all, I could hear the soft even breathing of sleepers beside me. Closing my eyes, I let myself drift into sleep, too.

CHAPTER 3
BENEATH THE STARS

A cool breeze was brushing my face as I woke. The sun was setting, and deep shadows were beginning to hide the landscape from view. As carefully as I could, I lifted one of the tamarisk branches so I could look up at the sky. A large hawk of some kind was circling overhead, its tail blazing like flame in the setting sun.

Then rustling sounds nearby told me my companions were also awake.

"What now?" I heard Mom ask.

"Boy, am I hungry," said Garek.

Celestia yawned, then said, "This is our biggest problem—food. My dad assumed we'd find an outpost soon after our GAP-crossing, so we have only a couple of days' supply, if we eat lightly to stretch it."

I nodded, "We had to leave enough at the cave for Jon and Martina because their stores were running low."

"All I can offer you now is some dried venison and fruit-leather," sighed Celestia.

"Well, that's better than nothing."

I could tell by her slight laugh that Mom was trying to make the best of our situation. Smiling at her gratefully, I helped hand out small portions to each of us.

"Do you think we've ended up in the wrong place?" I asked, as we were finishing our meager meal.

"It's hard to tell at this point," Celestia sighed. "If we could focus on a person, we might have better luck."

"But that's a power of the younger sibling, isn't it?" said Mom.

"And all of us are first-born."

"I bet Jon didn't even think of that."

"Well, he had a lot to figure out—what with people so scattered and no way to contact most of them, especially the children."

"Yeah, Mom, and most of the adults in the camp were first-borns, anyway."

"Except Martina," added Garek.

"And Dad needed her to help locate her uncle, the Rebel leader. So, I guess he really had no other choice," Celestia sighed.

By now, night had fully fallen, and pinpoint stars were beginning to appear in the dark sky. It was getting chilly since the sunset, so I stood, rubbed my arms with my hands, and pulled my jacket out of my packsack. Then I let my long blond hair drop out of its ponytail, so the back of my neck wouldn't feel the chill breath of air sweeping up from the valley below us.

"Let's see if we can get high enough for a view," said Celestia. "Better pack up everything. Night will be the best time to travel."

Soon we were moving out of our rock-cleft shelter. It felt like leaving the safety of a home we might never see again. I shook my head, trying to keep such negative thoughts out of my mind. This was no time to let my mood slide downward.

Once we'd left the cleft, we found a narrow game trail angling up a slope, traversing the side of the ridge. Fortunately, a full moon soon rose, so we could watch better for stones and other obstacles in our path. As often as I could, I stopped to look up at the stars and see if I could get any bearings. The moon was a mixed blessing, though, for its light was washing out the light of many of the stars.

"I think I see the Big Dipper," said Mom suddenly.

"Where?" Celestia and I asked together.

She stepped closer to me. "See that square of stars?" She pointed, and my eyes finally found the shape she indicated. "Follow the top edge stars off to your right. Can you see a single star?"

"I can see a smaller square just below."

"That's the Little Dipper," Mom smiled. "The North Star is at the tip of its handle, but it's quite dim and harder to see than it was in my time."

"So now we know we're looking north," said Garek. "That's a start, at least."

Then we began trudging slowly again. Although we knew which way we were moving, it didn't help much. The moonlight made everything look silvery, and I reached out to touch the rock wall to my right. There was still a little residual heat from the day, and it helped to warm my chilled fingers.

Suddenly, my toe hit a rock in the path and I stumbled forward. Before I knew it, my feet were sliding in loose rock and sand, and I was dropping off the edge of the trail. All this took place in a matter of seconds, but I felt the sensation of time slowing down and my life flashing before my eyes. 'You're a goner,' my mind told me.

Desperately, I tried to grab at anything my hands could find. Rocks and sharp sticks cut into my palms, but then one of my hands found a small tree growing at an angle from the cliff. Clinging with both hands, I shouted, "Help!"

"Annie!" Mom screamed.

"I can't hold on for long! My hands are slipping!"

My feet were dangling below me in empty darkness. I wasn't sure if this was better than seeing how far I might fall—or worse. Then a large shape loomed at the cliff edge, and I heard my father's voice:

"Stay calm, Annemarie. I can almost reach you."

But a rain of sand and gravel began to fall onto my head as he tried to move closer.

"I'm slipping!" I cried.

"If you swing one hand up toward me, I can grab it." How could he keep his voice sounding so cool and collected?

"But if I let one hand go, I might not be able to hold on."

"Believe in yourself, Annemarie. You can do it."

Gritting my teeth, and waiting for the fall I thought was inevitable, I gripped the tree tighter with my left hand, and swung my right up into the darkness. Immediately, a large, strong hand grabbed my wrist.

"Hold my wrist, too, so we have a double grip."

Slowly he began to pull me toward him, and soon I had to let go of my little tree. Once he pulled me close enough, he threw his other arm around my waist and heaved me onto the trail. It seemed like only seconds as he pulled me, and then I lay panting in his arms, tears streaming down my dirt-covered cheeks. I could hear him humming a tune.

'This is my Daddy,' my mind said in wonder.

"Oh, thank God!" I heard Mom's shaky voice say. Then I realized she was holding my hand. "Are you hurt, Annie?"

"I don't think so." Gingerly, I stood—and except for a twinge in my right knee, everything seemed in working order. Then I pulled Garek to me and hugged him tight. "Whew! That was close. Thanks, Dad."

He smiled that crooked smile of his. "No problem."

Looking into his eyes, I could see what had attracted my mother and Martina to him, back in Salien—before I was born. He seemed to radiate a kind of warmth, a blend of friendly, good humor and animal magnetism which was hard to explain, and even harder to resist. But I could also see why someone like Mom, who'd spent much of her life as a loner, felt overwhelmed by him.

"I guess I'd better watch where I'm going, instead of star-gazing," I said, to break the spell.

As we began moving again, I walked more carefully. After watching my feet for quite awhile, I looked up to find we were at a switchback. The trail turned back on itself and around a corner of the cliff. Suddenly a wide vista appeared.

"What is that?" came Celestia's surprised voice.

"I'm not sure," Mom replied. "Garek, you know more about Earth cities in this Thirty-first Century. Any ideas?"

He stepped closer and shook his head. "I haven't seen anything like this for a long time."

On the wide plain below us were thousands of lights. Some were arranged in long lines and rows, some straight and others curving. There were even lights moving along them. Closer to the horizon, the lights were arranged in grids, while some shone from tall buildings.

"It looks like Denver," I said, my voice full of awe and surprise.

"You're right," cried Mom. "But more like Twenty-first Century Denver."

"How can that be?"

"I don't know for sure," sighed Celestia.

"To me it looks a bit like Salien did, when I was working there," Garek added.

"When we met?"

"Uh-well, I guess so, Ginna."

I saw him try to reach for her hand, but she stepped away.

Suddenly I heard Celestia give a gasp, "I think we've fallen into a Time Well!"

"A what?"

"A Time Well, Ginna."

"You mean like one of those 'Wormholes' we heard about in Sci-fi stories?" I asked.

"Not exactly," Celestia replied. "Those are usually out in space. A Time Well is limited to one planet."

"How could this have happened?" Garek asked, stepping closer to me as Celestia continued:

"I have no idea. What we need to do now is find out where—and when—we are. Then perhaps we can find a way back out of here."

Silence loomed, as each of us retreated into our own thoughts. My dad was the one who finally spoke:

"It seems to me the only way to learn anything is to head down to that city there. At least then we can figure out where we are."

He set his hand on my shoulder as he spoke, and I found it comforting. Suddenly I realized I *was* thankful to have him with us. Not just because he was a man and my long-lost father, but more because he seemed to have a quiet strength about him, keeping me from falling into panic. Then I knew he wasn't the kind of man who'd force himself on you, despite what Mom seemed to be thinking. Along with his magnetism, there was a quiet confidence which showed itself in restraint. Now I could see Celestia smiling at him, and realized she was probably feeling the same thing.

We continued along the trail, looking now for a way down onto the plain below us.

***

The sun was rising behind us, just peeking over the ridge. Now we knew for sure we were heading west toward the city.

"This can't be Denver," said Mom. "We'd be facing east as we came out of the mountains."

"That's right," Garek nodded.

"Look!" Mom cried suddenly. "What's that?"

We all followed where she was pointing to the west. The orange light of the early morning sun seemed to glint off a body of water out there.

"Now I know where we are," Mom said. "I think that's the Great Salt Lake—and this is Salt Lake City."

"Where's that?" Celestia asked.

"In our time it's called Salien," whispered Garek.

"But whose time are we in right now?"

"Well, Annemarie," he sighed. "In my time that lake was all gone. It gradually evaporated away. So, we're in *my* past, for sure."

"We won't know exactly until we get down there, though, so we'd better keep moving," said Celestia.

"Maybe we can get some more food there," said Mom.

Garek laughed his characteristic explosive laugh. "That's the best thought we've heard all night."

***

The sun was climbing to its highest point in the sky as we finally reached the city. I was feeling tired, hungry, and discouraged. My knee was beginning to hurt more with each step, but I didn't want to complain or slow the others down.

'Why do things seem to always go wrong for me?' I wondered. I knew I was just having a pity party, but there was nothing I could do to stop myself. As I thought back over my life, it seemed to be a long steady downward spiral—of one bad choice after another.

Just to get my mind off myself, I turned to Celestia walking beside me, and struck up a conversation. "Tell me about your life, Celestia. You've heard a lot of my story already."

"That's true. I suppose it *is* my turn," she smiled.

I glanced in Mom's direction, hoping she wouldn't hear too much about how Celestia and I had met in Denver.

I felt better when she began, "I was born in a small mountain valley town in western North America. When winter came, we moved to Celeton, staying with my uncles for a couple of years. This was when my parents and Uncle Jael made their trip to the Fountain."

"Along with Mom and my Uncle Danny 'within' them."

"That's right. But I was too young to remember any of it—either their leaving me for the weeks their journey took, or their return to us in Celeton.

"I do remember, as I grew out of toddlerhood that my grandmother, Irina, seemed to come visit whenever she could. Raina lived with her, and she and Jael were good friends.

"This was when my parents finally found a small house for us. It was on the edge of town, which we all liked. I could run in the fields along the river and wander the residential streets, wonderful freedom after living in a flat in the center-city. Mom loved all the plants and trees around us, and I knew Dad liked working outdoors in our garden whenever he could.

"The most exciting part for me was when I was able to start school. Here on Earth, schools still had some books, in addition to the computing terminals that were prevalent everywhere. I loved to read, but my favorite subject was natural science. Being in the outdoors was my favorite classroom, as I did plot studies of the various vegetation types around our area, or studied the life-cycles and habitats of local animals.

"Another thing we all liked about our home was how the city lights were hidden behind the low hills to our west. This meant we had some magnificent views of the stars. Dad, especially, would sit and gaze at them for hours. As I grew older, he began to tell me stories of when he'd voyaged from Rubicon to Terres with his parents. Other times, he and Mom related some of their adventures finding their way from Terres to Earth.

"On the colder nights, we'd all wrap ourselves in a large blanket and snuggle to keep warm. Often, Dad or Mom would sing a song they'd learned from a friend:

Voice of your radiance, speaking of brilliance,
Language of fullness, streaming everywhere.
Universe dreaming songs of including
Sons of creation, waiting on the dawn.

Far from discerning words of our yearning,
Dreaming of freedom, calling into the deep.
Longing for union, creation's communion,
Breath of redemption, revive the heart's domain.

Look how far beyond the northern star
Your song still echoes thru the void.
Your music flows where angels long to go,
Worlds of wonder, glistening in the dark.

"But this idyllic life was not to last much longer. When I was about eighteen Earth Years old, the war started. No one was sure exactly how it began, but soon ships from System Planets around the Galaxy were converging on Earth.

"At first, they claimed to be 'discovering our planet' as though it hadn't been known before. Mom told me how all her life the System denied Earth's existence, 'So now they find they're interested in us after all, but they have to keep on pretending they didn't know about us before.'

" 'Why are they interested in us?' I asked.

"She shrugged. 'Maybe Dad knows—I don't.'

"By this time, officials from the huge 'Diplomatic Ships' had come to the largest cities of our planet. Every leader in each part of the Earth was told they must obey the System or die. Most surrendered and let the System take over.

"Not all did, however. In a few places where Rebels were stronger, fierce battles were fought, both on the ground and in the sky. Fields and forests which were green and fruitful were laid waste. Then Patrols of soldiers began to scour the cities, searching out Believers. Those they took were never seen again, and those of us who could, fled to the wild places."

My mother joined us just as Celestia was saying this.

"So that's how the System got established here on Earth. I was wondering," she said.

"Yes, it all happened in the time you were gone, after Jon took you and Danny back."

"That was about twenty-five years—in my time, at least."

"Here, too, I guess, because that's how old I am now," said Celestia.

"Why do people hate Believers so much?" I asked.

"I'm not sure. Of course, my view is just one small piece of the picture. But I think it has to do with the way we think of the True King as being the ultimate authority in the Universe. Humans don't seem to like anyone or anything to be more powerful than themselves."

"Some humans, anyway." Garek joined us. "Personally, I'm not sure I like the idea of being where 'the credit stops'."

"What does that mean?" I asked.

"I think it's sort of like our saying, 'the buck stops here'," said Mom. "You know, it means there's no one else to blame. You're the one responsible for whatever the problem or outcome is."

"Okay, I think I see."

"Somehow the System wants us to believe *they* have all the answers," added Celestia. "At least that's what Mom often said. Anything which doesn't support this idea is an enemy to the System. So, things like Believers, The Book, the idea of an all-powerful God—those are all bad to the System."

Garek was looking at her closely as she said this. I wondered what was going on in his mind—if any of this was making sense to him. "You know, most of my life there was no System here on Earth," he said quietly. "When it came, I was close to retiring from my career, so I could mostly ignore it and keep on living my life as before."

"Until we showed up," I sighed.

He smiled slightly. "Partly true. But I've been a reader of books all my life, and I still hold many old ideas. You could say my mind wasn't as vulnerable to the System because of that. I just tried to keep a low profile, and not draw any attention to myself."

"In my time, we called that 'flying under the radar'."

"I've heard of radar, Ginna," he laughed, "In my reading. It was a way to detect objects by bouncing radio waves off them."

"Yes," Mom nodded. "And then they began to develop planes that could avoid detection by flying close enough to the ground to mess up the radar waves."

"I also read about planes with certain shapes, so the waves don't bounce right, making them 'invisible' to the radar," he added.

"That's right. You know more about my time than I realized."

All of us stopped walking then and gazed toward the city's skyline. Garek reached for Mom's hand, but she ignored him. I wished she'd really look at him and see what a good man he was. But then I wondered if she'd even believe me. I didn't have a great track record with good judgment of men.

CHAPTER 4
THE NIGHT CITY

By the next nightfall, we were deep into a residential area of the city. Signs we read told us this area was called Bountiful. The homes did seem to be large with well-kept lawns. We didn't see many people around, though there were some groundcars parked in front of most of the dwellings.

Lamps on tall poles were shedding light on the streets around us as we continued trudging on. Gradually, the buildings began to be shabbier and multi-storied with high, dingy windows.

"What on Earth is this?" asked Celestia.

"Looks like what we called a slum," said Mom.

"Well, it sure is older than the area we just came through."

"Right, Dad. We're getting into what people in my time called the Inner City."

Just at that moment, a group of five young men stepped in front of us. We weren't near one of those street-lights, so we didn't see them standing in an alley to our left. It was apparent they intended to stop our progress.

"Give us your money," one growled.

"Yeah, looks like you must have *something*, with those nice clothes," another added.

I never considered my outdoor pants and tunic anything special. Perhaps my father's clothing looked richer to them.

"We have no money," Dad said, keeping his voice calm and even.

Suddenly, one of the others pulled a knife out and grabbed me. "Yeah, right! Now hand over everything in your pockets, or she dies."

My heart was pounding so hard it made my head spin. All I could see was my dad and the others pulling everything out of their packsacks and pockets and piling it on the ground at my feet. Besides our clothes and nearly-empty water-bottles, the only things in the pile were what was left of our food—a couple of strips of fruit-leather—and a few plastic credit tokens from Dad's pocket. We were already wearing most of the clothing we brought with us.

One of the young men picked up the tokens curiously. "What's this stuff?"

"That's money where I come from," said Dad. "Probably won't be much use to you here."

"Cut the crap." The young man threw the tokens down.

"Yeah!" added another. "Where're you from, outer space?"

"Uh—you could say that." I was surprised to hear Mom speak up.

"Please believe us," Celestia added. "That's really all we have."

One of the youths grabbed her then. "Maybe I should just strip-search you."

She screamed, and at the same time I heard her tunic rip.

Suddenly a bright flashing light came toward us down the street, and the hands gripping me were gone, along with the knife at my throat. In an instant, our attackers all disappeared. A loud siren sounded briefly, and then a groundcar stopped nearby. A man in a dark blue uniform got out and walked toward us, and I could see another one still in the vehicle.

"Are you all right, Ma'am?" He directed his question to me.

I found I could only nod, still trying to catch my breath and rubbing the tender spot where the knife had slightly pricked my skin. Dad handed me a handkerchief, which I pressed against the trickle of blood.

"Are you hurt?" I heard Mom's worried voice ask.

"No, it's just a scratch—really."

"What happened?" the uniformed man asked.

"Some young men jumped us and demanded all our

money," said Dad. I was thankful he took over the spokes-man role, as I felt too shaken to speak.

"That's typical for this neighborhood," the man nod-ded. "You shouldn't be out here after dark."

"We didn't know, sir," said Mom. "We aren't from around here."

"Where are you headed?"

There were a few seconds of awkward silence. None of us knew enough about the city to give any answer. Then I heard Dad's deep, comforting voice again:

"We were hoping to find some kind of lodging in a homeless shelter. As Ginna said, we aren't from around here and don't know anyone here in the city."

"But what brought you here?" Now the officer was beginning to sound suspicious.

Again, Dad came to our rescue. "I worked in the Sali—the Salt Lake City Federal Building several years ago. At that time there was a hostel nearby for workers who had no permanent homes."

I had no idea what he was talking about but hoped the officer might find the story convincing. Apparently, it did make some sense to him, for he finally said, "Well, there is a 'Y' down near the Capitol. They may still have a couple of beds open tonight. I'd better take you there in the squad car, though. That neighborhood is as dangerous as this one."

As he led us toward the vehicle he called the 'squad

car', I saw Dad smile at me reassuringly. "It'll be okay," he whispered and patted my shoulder.

Soon the four of us were squeezed into a seat obviously designed for three. None of us said a word as the car began to move slowly through the tunnel-like streets. The tall, old-looking buildings seemed to be closing in on us, and I tried not to fall into panic.

"In my world, the presence of uniformed officers was not a good sign," Celestia whispered.

"It must be different in this time, because my dad doesn't seem too concerned," I replied in her ear.

Then brighter lights appeared before us, and the street widened into a tree-lined boulevard. Down a slight hill, loomed a wide building with a beautiful lighted dome rising from its center.

"Ah, there's the Capitol," said Dad.

"Yes, sir," said one of the officers from the front seat. As he turned, I noticed he had dark, tightly-curled hair peeking out from under his hat. "Have you seen it before?"

"Long ago, when I worked here," he replied. I saw him wink at Mom as he said this. They both knew his 'long ago' was actually in the future.

Just then, the car turned left onto a side street and stopped in front of a three story, brick building. Above the double front doors was a sign that read, 'YMCA.'

"This place hasn't changed much," Dad added. I wondered if this was true or he was just adlibbing.

"Never does," said the officer seated on the right. He was getting out of the car by now, and opened the vehicle's right rear door. "I'll go in with you to make sure they have rooms. We don't want you to be stuck on the streets alone all night." He seemed to almost smile at me as he said this.

Once we stepped inside the doors, we were hit with an old, musty smell. I felt my nose begin to tickle, and sneezed. The lights were not very bright, but soon I made out a dark wooden desk ahead of us. Behind it a dark-haired young man was seated, but instead of black or brown, his hair was blue.

"What can I do for you, Officer Simms?"

"Hi, Timon," said our escort. "These folks are new to the city and have no safe place to stay."

"And no money either, I take it?"

Officer Simms glanced at us, and we shrugged. "They were getting robbed when I found them."

"No worries," the blue-haired Timon smiled. "They can earn their keep with cleaning work. Let's see, one man, three women. I take it none of you are married?"

We all shook our heads.

"The three gals will have to take a double room, and one gets the couch. The man can bunk in the men's dormitory."

"That will be fine," Dad smiled. "Just show us how to get there."

"No baggage?"

"Just what little is left in our packsacks," I said, speaking up for the first time.

"I'll need to inspect them, if you don't mind," said Timon. "Can't have any weapons or illegals in here, you see."

We nodded, and stood silently as he rummaged through each of our bags.

"Looks like you've been camping," he smiled. "Out in the desert?"

"Yes, sir," said Mom. "Somehow, we got lost, though. Next thing we knew, we could see the Great Salt Lake."

"Yeah, that's hard to miss," grinned Timon. "Well, it looks like you're all good to go. Sir, the dorm is up those stairs and to your right. I'll take the women to their room." As he rose, he nodded to Officer Simms, who turned and headed toward the door.

"Thanks for your help, sir," I called after him.

He turned back, smiled, and nodded to me. I noticed how piercing his black eyes looked in his dark brown face—they really stood out despite his dark uniform.

***

Once we were seated on the bed in our room, I finally could catch my breath. "I thought Earth in your time was dangerous, Celestia."

"Well, there was stuff like this in our time, too," said Mom.

"Yeah, I had to stay at the 'Y' in Denver for awhile before I could find an apartment," I added. "It was okay as long as I didn't have to go out after dark."

Mom gave me a hard look. "I never knew about that."

"There are lots of things you don't know, Mom—and probably don't want to know, either."

Then she turned and looked down at the worn carpet, and I could sense her drawing away from us. I decided I'd better change the subject:

"Can we get anything to eat here?"

"I think they have a soup kitchen downstairs," said Mom. "I smelled food when we were climbing the stairs."

"I'm famished."

"Me too, Celestia. What about you, Mom?"

"I guess it would be best if we stick together. Just watch carefully, so we can find our way back to our room."

"Okay, Mom. Maybe we should leave a trail of bread-crumbs?"

The two of us began to laugh. "If only we had some bread," Mom added.

"What?" Celestia asked, looking confused.

"Oh, it's just an old fairy tale," I said. "About two children trying not to get lost in the woods."

"Uh—okay."

"Yeah, I hope there isn't a witch in the kitchen who wants to bake us for dinner," Mom giggled.

"I'm still clueless," said Celestia. "I hope you two aren't getting hysterical on me."

"Don't worry, we'll tell you the whole story some-time," Mom smiled. "Right now I'm too hungry."

A short time later, we found our way down to the soup kitchen. I was very glad to see Dad sitting at one of the long trestle tables, with a steaming bowl of soup and a plate of rolls in front of him.

"Go get yourselves a bowl," he smiled. "I have plenty bread for all of us."

Soon we joined him. The soup seemed to be mostly broth, with some kind of grain, different vegetables, and a few tiny bits of meat. The person serving called it 'beef barley' soup. I would've called it 'barely beef' myself. Still, it was warm, and the bread was good and filling.

None of us said much until we finished our meals.

"Well, *now* what do we do?" sighed Mom.

"I suggest we try to get a good night's sleep," smiled Dad.

"I mean after that," she replied sharply.

"Take it easy, Mom."

"I'm sorry. I guess my nerves are just frazzled."

"Dad, did you know this place was really here?" I asked. "Or was it just a lucky guess?"

"A bit of both. I knew most large cities have homeless shelters or hostels of some kind. I think these YMCA's used to be common in the Twentieth Century."

"You were right." I reached over and patted his arm. It was beginning to feel more natural to call him Dad now.

"But we do need to try to come up with some kind of plan. We can't just stay here forever."

"Annemarie's right. The 'Y' is meant to be a temporary lodging," he nodded.

"But we have no idea 'when' we are," sighed Celestia, speaking at last.

"I found a magazine that I think may be current." He held up a booklet with a shiny cover. On the front were pictures of people who seemed to be dressed in quite fancy clothes. "The date of this issue is 'May, 2123'."

"So that's about 125 years after our time," said Mom.

"And probably over 900 Standard Years before mine and Garek's," said Celestia.

"Isn't there any way to cross a Time-GAP back to our own time?" I asked.

"Whose own time, mine or yours?" smiled Dad.

"Sorry, but I can't get to either one just crossing blind," said Celestia. "I need coordinates."

"But when Martina and I were looking for you three in Tornatoh, we crossed blind from Garek's house to the prison."

"Not quite blind, Ginna," she answered. "Mom was guiding the crossing by concentrating on me, and that wasn't a Time-GAP."

"Oh, yeah. And we don't have anyone with us who can guide do we?"

I could tell by her voice Mom was getting close to tears. "Does this mean we're stuck here?"

"I didn't say that, Ginna. I'm not sure yet what I can do, but I won't give up trying to figure something out. We need to learn more about this place. Then perhaps we'll find a clue to help us."

"At least we know we're in Salt Lake City," Mom nodded. "And Garek knows a little about the city, right?"

He smiled. "Well, I know its future, anyway. A few things are familiar—like the capitol building."

"Yeah, that was lucky. It seemed to take away some of the police officers' suspicions."

"Wasn't there an ancient temple of some kind in this city?" asked Mom.

"How did you know that?" he asked.

"I was here 'in' Martina, remember?"

Dad suddenly blushed. "Oh, yeah," he laughed. "How could I forget that?"

"It's what caused this entire trip in the first place, Dad."

"Yeah, I guess so," he sighed.

"I wonder if there's some force that's drawn us to this place where it all started?" whispered Mom.

Dad reached over and took her hand in his. I was surprised, but thankful, when she didn't pull away from him this time. "Well, like I said. I think we'd better try to get some sleep. Sometimes things make more sense in the light of day," he added.

We all stood then and walked out of the dining area. At the door, he paused. "My dorm is to the left."

"We go the other way and upstairs to the next floor," I said.

I could tell he was hesitant to let go of Mom's hand, so I took Celestia's elbow and pulled her with me down the hallway. "Let's let them have some time alone," I whispered.

She nodded, and we started up the stairs. Part of me was curious enough to want to look back and see if she'd let him at least give her a hug, but I resisted.

Once we got to our room, both of us sat down on the bed and sighed. Then I had to laugh. "This reminds me of when we sat down on the bed in my Denver hotel."

"Yeah, I was thinking the same thing. It seems like such a long time ago now."

"Well, it actually is, even in this time. And in our own lives, a lot has happened, whatever time you choose to count in. Sometimes this is all too mind-boggling for me," I sighed. "I wish I could just go back home."

My voice began to crack, and she reached across to pat my shoulder. "Somehow we'll get back."

"Back to my time, or forward to yours?"

"I can't say right now. But one thing I do believe, the Lord has a plan here somewhere—even if we can't see it."

"I sure hope you're right, Celestia. Besides, I'm not even sure which time to call 'home' anymore."

Tears were beginning to slide down my cheeks now.

"Annemarie, I'm so sorry I brought you here. I

shouldn't have messed with your life." She hugged me tightly.

"No, don't say that. If you hadn't come, I'd probably be a suicide by now. I was just climbing into the hotel window, you know. At least this way, I still have a second chance at life."

"Never give up, Annemarie. Please keep believing and hoping."

We sat for what seemed a long time, until the door finally opened slowly. Mom didn't say anything as she came in, and I couldn't tell by her face whether she was happy with how things went saying good-night.

CHAPTER 5
THE CITY BY DAY

Early the next morning, we all woke to the sound of a bell ringing.

"That must mean breakfast," I yawned. "Just like the 'Y' in Denver." Another long yawn covered my voice entirely.

I sat up and stretched, not feeling nearly as stiff as I did from sleeping on mats in the cave. Sleeping on a couch hadn't been bad at all. "How was the bed, Mom?" I asked.

"It was fine," she shrugged. "I know I'm still spoiled by having a real bed back home." Her voice broke, and she sighed. "Well, I used to. I don't know where home is now."

"Let's go down and get some food," Celestia finally spoke. "Hopefully that will help our brains start working."

None of us said anything else as we got back into our traveling clothes. For the night, all we'd had to sleep in was underwear, but that hadn't been as cold as I'd expected. This place evidently had a good heat system, and I smiled inwardly as I remembered comments Dad had made about missing central heat. He'd probably enjoyed a warm night's sleep for a change, even if he was in a large, open men's dormitory.

When we reached the kitchen area, there was a line at the serving window, so we joined the end of it. The servers were handing out plates piled with some steaming, fluffy yellow stuff.

"What's that?" Celestia whispered to me.

"Scrambled eggs, I think."

"Where do they get so many? Eggs are rare in my world, especially after we fled the cities. Occasionally, we find a few bird eggs and boil them. But it would take thousands of the tiny wild bird eggs to make these heaps of yellow."

"In my time there were farms raising thousands of chickens, collecting their eggs, and selling them by the dozen in the markets," I smiled.

She shook her head in disbelief, never having seen anything like this.

By this time, we'd reached the head of the line and were handed plates. Beside the eggs was a strip of fatty meat and a piece of toasted bread.

"Typical breakfast of my time," I smiled. "Eggs, bacon and toast."

Soon we found seats at one of the long tables and began to taste the food. Before I knew it, my plate was empty.

"That was amazing," I sighed, pushing back from the table.

"You can probably go back for seconds," I heard a voice behind me say. Turning, I saw it was Dad, with a heaping plate of eggs and two slices of bacon.

"Are you sure?"

"Oh, there's plenty more where this came from, and the line is nearly gone. Go ahead."

I glanced at Celestia, not wanting to go alone, and she stood up. As we walked back to the line, I also realized this was a good ploy to give Dad and Mom some more time alone.

So, we took our time getting to the end of the line, and even let a few late-comers go ahead of us. Both of us kept trying not to look toward the table to see what was going on, but we did glance now and then. The two of them seemed to be smiling as they talked, though neither was making a move to hold hands or anything.

When we got back with our plates, they were just eating the last of their food.

"Pretty good breakfast for a soup kitchen, huh?" said Dad.

"I have no complaints," Celestia nodded. "But I've never seen so many eggs in my life."

"Really," he laughed. But then his grin faded. "I guess your lives have been pretty rough sometimes, huh?"

We both nodded, and as I looked at Celestia, I could tell she was really missing her parents. In fact, tears sprang to her eyes. "Why do I suddenly feel like a lost child?" she murmured.

Dad pulled her into a hug. "There now, Celestia. We'll take care of you."

She pulled back, apparently embarrassed he thought her a child needing his care. But the concern in his eyes showed he meant well.

"Well, what should we do now?" Mom finally spoke, after an awkward silence.

"First, we have to take our turn washing dishes," said Dad. "That's how we're paying for our room and board here."

"Oh, yeah," I sighed. "Everything has its price, doesn't it?"

***

There must have been fifty or sixty people staying at the 'Y', based on the number of dishes we washed from breakfast. But it helped to be doing the task together. As we worked and talked, I began to appreciate the kinship I had with these three who weren't from my time or circumstances. It was good not to be alone.

Once the chores were finished, we decided to walk around this part of the city, during the daylight when it would be safer.

As I'd noticed last night, the boulevard going up to what Dad called the Capitol was wide and lined with trees.

On green lawns in front of the gleaming white building, there were beds of many-colored flowers.

"This reminds me of the gardens at the Temple of the Way in Tornatoh," said Mom suddenly.

We all looked at her curiously, and then realized none of us had seen that place, only she and her brother Danny, when they were 'within' Martina and Jael.

"I wish I could have seen it," Celestia sighed.

"You were only a baby," she smiled. "You wouldn't remember it, even if you did."

"What was it like, Mom?" I asked.

"Well, it seemed very impressive at the time. The fountains shot high into the air, with many bright colors moving in time to beautiful music."

"I never made it to Tornatoh's Temple," Dad said then. "I only lived there a couple of years after I retired. Sounds like I missed a spectacular sight."

"Oh, it *looked* awesome," Mom nodded. "But it was just for show. It had no real power to heal anyone's body or soul. It was only—well—it wasn't the True Fountain. That was completely different."

"In what way?" he asked, and I saw him reach out to touch her shoulder. She didn't pull away, and I smiled to myself.

"It wasn't much more than a pool in the cleft of a rock. But the water made us feel—it's hard to explain—restored, whole—things like that."

"Maybe we were at the right place in that first rocky cliff, and didn't know it," I sighed.

"No, I don't think it was the same spring. That water didn't feel or taste like what I remember from the Fountain."

Suddenly I wanted to smack myself on the head. "Of course! If we've gone back nine hundred years, maybe the True Fountain hasn't even appeared yet."

"Or if it *is* there, it hasn't been discovered."

"Could be, Celestia."

"Maybe we'll be the ones to discover it," cried Mom.

But Celestia shook her head. "I don't see how. We don't have any idea what desert to look in."

"We have to figure out where Tornatoh is first," Mom continued. "I know the Fountain was east of there, past two large lakes and a range of high mountains."

"But that's almost a millennium in the future," I sighed. "The terrain may be entirely different now."

"Maybe not totally different," Dad spoke up at last. "Perhaps if we can find some maps, we can do some research."

By this time, I noticed Mom letting Dad hold her hand. "Do you remember telling Martina about an ancient temple here in Salien?" she said. "It should be around here somewhere, if this is the same city, shouldn't it?"

Now it was his turn to cry out in surprise. "Of course, why didn't I think of that? The Morotani Temple was very ancient in my time. It must be here somewhere."

"Maybe we can find some answers there," I said excitedly.

Soon we were asking passersby if any of them knew of this temple. Many shook their heads, but one nodded and said, "Look for the signs saying 'Temple Square', just a few blocks southwest of here. It used to be a popular place, but not so many go there anymore."

Following these directions, we finally managed to find the square with its many old, tall trees. In the center was a towering grey stone building with peaked towers.

Ivy was climbing the walls surrounding the compound. There didn't seem to be any gates to enter the grounds on the side we came to first. As we walked around the perimeter, I heard Mom telling Dad this reminded her of trying to find a way into the temple in Tornatoh.

At last, we came to a break in the wall, with a large, heavy-looking set of doors. As we raised the massive metal knocker, a window slid open in the wall to our right.

"What do you want?" snapped an unfriendly voice.

"We were wondering if we could come in to see the temple," I said.

"Are you followers of the Chosen?"

"We're Believers," I whispered.

"Wrong answer," he barked, and closed the window abruptly.

"No wonder this place isn't so popular anymore," sighed Celestia.

"Actually, it's this way in my time, too," Dad said. "No one but the initiated are allowed to enter."

"How does one get initiated?" asked Mom.

"Evidently, they aren't looking for new members right now," Dad chuckled softly. "Otherwise, he would have told us."

"So now what?" I sighed.

"I suggest we look for a library. Maybe they'll have maps that can help us," he smiled.

"A what? I've never heard of a 'library'," said Celestia.

"It's a place where they keep thousands of books and other information," I smiled.

"A place full of books? Wow, those sure don't exist in my time."

"Pretty rare in my life, too," added Dad. "But I'm hoping that in 2123 they still have them. Let's see what we can find. Usually, a library will be near the city center."

Once again, we began asking people near us for directions to a library. The first two or three just shook their heads and walked on, and I began to be fearful books were being banned here, too. But the next person we met actually smiled and said, "Of course! It's just five blocks south of here. Follow State Street down to 400 South."

As we were walking south on the street the man indicated, Dad stopped for a moment in front of a large brick and stone building. Above the door were the words 'Federal Building.'

"Wow, it looks much like it will in my time," he said. "Do you recognize it, Ginna?"

She looked up at the three-story building for a few moments before she spoke. "That's where you and Martina worked on the Resource Project, isn't it?"

"Yes. Actually, it's where we *will* work on it in a few hundred years."

We walked a couple more blocks and came around a corner. I saw Celestia's jaw drop, as a beautiful white building with large columns met our view. Climbing beside me on a wide set of majestic stairs, she murmured, "I'm amazed books are so revered here and kept in such a wonderful place."

Inside, we came to a large wooden desk, where a smiling attendant asked if we needed any help.

"Do you have a map room of antique paper maps?" Dad asked.

"Yes, sir. Take the lift to the second floor, and when you come out, it will be to your left."

"Thank you," I said, as we moved toward the lift doors.

Along the walls of the room were shelves reaching from floor to ceiling, filled with books of all sizes and shapes. The smell of the paper was like perfume to me. Suddenly, I saw Celestia stop and run her fingers along the spines of some of the books. Most were bound with some kind of shiny paper, but there were older ones that looked like leather.

"I think I'm in Heaven," she whispered and smiled at me.

"Gosh, Celestia," I said, "I guess I never realized how special books are to you."

"You often don't know the true value of something until it's gone," she sighed.

Dad stepped up beside her and was also caressing some of the book covers. "I know exactly what you mean," he smiled.

Then we moved into the lift. When its doors slid open on the second floor, there was a large room with glass windows just to our left. Inside were wide, shallow drawers, and in these were laid maps of many kinds. Labels on each drawer classified them by what section of the world they were in.

"Oh, my," I said. "There are so many. Where do we start?"

Dad smiled. "This will be new to me, working with all this paper. I'm more accustomed to digital files and touch-screens. Ginna, you and I know this city called Tornatoh was a three-day journey by groundcar from Celeton."

"Yes, but those city names aren't showing up in any of the indices," Mom said.

"Then let's think about the kind of climate and terrain you saw," he continued. "You were in a desert east of a high mountain range."

"Yes, and it seemed we walked for several days."

"Celeton and Salien weren't too far apart, were they? And we know that Salien is the city we're in now. Let's start from here."

He pulled out a map of western North America and pointed to where Salt Lake City was.

"The larger deserts here are west of the city," Mom observed. "If we go further west, there's a large mountain range. I wonder if that could be what Soren, our guide, called the Cruax Mountains. That would mean the city we started from was west of them."

"That's right," smiled Dad. He pointed toward some of the large cities along the western coast of the continent. "If you headed east out of any of these, you'd cross the mountains, and find desert on their east sides, because of the way the weather patterns are. It seems to me, they were still like this in my time, too."

"So, if any of these has a temple with fountains, and a tall tower that looks like Neptune Spire, then it will become Tornatoh."

"I'm so glad you remember all this, Mom," I sighed. "Without you, we'd really be lost."

"Well, I'm not sure how much help it will be. Even if we can find this temple, it won't get us to the Fountain."

"Now, Ginna," Celestia said softly. "Don't get discouraged. We'll just take each step as it comes to us."

"Yes, I've heard that before." She smiled then. "I remember a song we used to sing about the Lord leading us step-by-step. We need to keep trusting him."

I was surprised to hear my mother talk about remembering a song. "I used to sing that one a lot with David, Mom. I guess I never knew you liked it so much." But then I looked down and tried to blink back the tears beginning to come. It was still hard to think of David, and how I'd betrayed him.

"I'm going to take this map and see if they'll make a copy for us," said Dad, to break the silence. "Why don't you three get the rest of these put back in the proper drawers?"

He left the room, and we worked quietly, talking very little. I wished one of the others would talk so I could get my mind off David. But as it turned out, I was the one talking when Dad came back into the room.

I was telling Celestia how fortunate she was to have no love-complications in her life, "Perhaps you're the lucky one, after all."

He looked at us curiously as we suddenly stopped talking. I couldn't think of anything else to say, so I just shrugged. He was polite enough to smile and not ask any questions.

The sun was setting as we headed back toward the 'Y' to stay another night. There really was no other choice, and it wasn't such a bad place. The soup this night was some kind of poultry with white pieces of dough, like dumplings. It tasted better than it looked.

It didn't take me as long to fall asleep that night, so I guess all the fresh air and walking in the city helped. Also, my mind was less troubled, now that we were beginning to develop a semblance of a plan. I curled up on the bed next to Mom, since Celestia insisted it was her turn to sleep on the couch. I was just thankful for a soft place to lie, as the quiet sound of my roommates' breathing lulled me to sleep.

CHAPTER 6
OFFICER SIMMS

Breakfast the next morning was pancakes and some rolls of spicy ground sausage. I could tell by the look on her face Celestia had never seen food like this, so I quietly explained it to her as soon as we were seated.

As we ate and chatted, we wondered where Dad was—it wasn't like him to miss a meal. Just as we'd finished our plates, he walked in, smiling.

"What are you grinning about?" asked Mom. "You look much too pleased with yourself."

"Are you hungry, Dad? I could go get you a plate of pancakes."

"No thanks, daughter. I had breakfast with a friend."

"A what?" we all asked together.

"How can you know anyone in this place and time?" I added.

"We met him the first night we got here."

"Not one of those men who tried to rob us?"

"No, Ginna. I went out for an early walk and ran into Officer Simms."

"You mean the one who helped us."

He nodded and smiled at me. "He asked how you were doing, Annemarie."

"Me?"

"He seemed to find you attractive," he added.

I looked down at my empty plate, not knowing what to say.

"He was just going off night duty," continued Dad. "He suggested we all meet in the park by the Capitol after lunch. That way he can get some rest first."

"But what does he want?" Mom sounded suspicious.

"He'd like to show us around the city, and perhaps help us find a way to travel to Tacoma."

"Tacoma? Where's that?"

"It's one of those coastal cities we saw on the map yesterday. I think it may be the ancestor of Tornatoh. After all, they both start with a 'T'."

Once we'd done our dishwashing chores, we took our packsacks with our few belongings and set out for the Capitol. The day was not as sunny as yesterday, and the wind was brisk. We were thankful we had layers of clothing.

Once we came in sight of the domed building, I saw a dark-haired young man standing near one of the flower-beds. At first, I didn't recognize him without his uniform, but when he smiled and waved, I saw it was Officer Simms, the dark-eyed one who'd taken us to the YMCA.

"Hello, Darroch," called Dad.

'Darroch?' I thought. 'Oh, of course, that must be his first name.'

He was striding toward us and quickly shook Dad's hand. "Good to see you all again." He smiled at each of us, but his gaze rest longer on me. "I was going to suggest we visit here in the gardens, but it's a bit chilly today. How about we go inside?"

"In there?" I pointed to the impressive white building. "Is that allowed?"

"Of course," he smiled. "It belongs to the people of Utah, our state. There's no more United States of America. Now it's the United States of the World, but we got to keep our original state name."

As we walked up the stairs, which looked like some kind of fine stone, I tried to take in every sight at once. Massive ornate doors swung open, and once inside we walked right into a wide hallway with many paintings hanging on the wall. After a short walk, we entered a huge circular room with large murals painted on the walls. It almost made me dizzy trying to turn and take them all in.

"Wow! Look at that," cried Celestia, pointing up.

Following her gesture, I beheld a most amazing sight. The inside of the dome opened into this room, and the circular space soared above us, lighted by windows of many-colored glass, and more gold-covered decorations than I'd ever seen.

"This is the rotunda," Darroch said, nodding to us. "Almost every state capitol had one. But not all survived the Unification Wars."

"The what?" I asked.

"Here, come sit on these benches, and I'll try to catch you up on your history. You must be from very far away, like another planet, if you haven't heard of the Unification Wars."

Celestia and I glanced at each other, wondering what to say. His comment about 'another planet' seemed to be said as a joke—we hoped.

Then Mom spoke up, "I guess you could say we come from a very remote place."

Darroch just smiled back at her.

These benches he spoke of were actually well-cushioned couches, upholstered in green and gold fabric. Once again, I realized how much I missed these comforts. It sure beat sitting on rocks and logs. Dad sat down next to Ginna, and I didn't see her pulling away from him this time. Darroch guided Celestia and me to the opposite bench and sat down between us.

"So, what do you know about Salt Lake City?" he began. "I heard from Garek that you tried to visit the Temple yesterday."

"They didn't seem very friendly," I said quickly.

"No, things have changed since the war. There used to be a special display for visitors to tell about the Faith of the Chosen, and to explain the history of the Morotani and the Temple."

"What are they?" I asked. "Some sort of religious sect?"

"I guess you could call it that. Anyway, they withdrew behind their walls when the rest of the buildings in the square were destroyed. There used to be a beautiful concert hall with a fine pipe organ, but it's gone now." By the tone of Darroch's voice, I could tell he was sad about this loss.

"Please tell us more about the war," I said then.

He nodded and began, "About a hundred years ago, in the Twenty-first Century…"

I tensed at the mention of my own time, but said nothing.

"Countries were falling apart into ethnic splinter groups," he continued. "It seemed no one could get along with anyone else. Everyone was fighting someone. Governments came and went much too quickly to keep any order. The country we used to be—the United States of America—also began to fragment, as different states and regions of the country decided to pull out of the union and make their own governments.

"Just when it seemed the world was going to completely fall apart, a man named Tarshiesh came onto the scene. Somehow, he gained control of the media and computer networks. I don't know what it was about him, but people seemed to listen and follow him almost blindly. In a few years, he managed to get most of the groups fighting each other to join with him. With this new army, he began the War of Unification—battling any group which resisted joining his new United States of the World."

"Do you think he was the Anti-Christ that The Book mentions?" asked Celestia. "I've heard my parents and uncles talk of this sometimes."

"What book?" Darroch looked confused.

"Perhaps in this time you still call it the Bible," Mom said softly.

Then he smiled. "Ah, yes, I know it well. A lot of people thought Tarshiesh was the Anti-Christ. But there were many others who were called 'Anti-Christ' through the ages, from the Roman Emperor Nero, who reigned over two thousand years ago, to some of the dictators of the Twentieth Century, which was only two hundred years ago."

"Like Hitler and Stalin?" I put in.

"Seems like I've heard some of those names," Darroch shrugged. "Many of them persecuted all forms of religion, but this is where Tarshiesh was different. He wanted all the religions to merge together and learn to cooperate. 'Each is a different path up the same mountain,' he said."

I saw Dad looking at Mom as she shook her head and said, "No, that's not quite true. Almost all religions claim to show people how to find their way to God."

"Isn't that what he meant by climbing the same mountain?" Dad was sounding puzzled.

"Please, let me finish," she sighed. "Every religion says that except Christianity. Christians believe God reached down to us, when his Son was born here on Earth. We couldn't find our way to God, no matter how many different 'paths' we tried, so he came down and made a 'ladder' for us."

"So that's what you truly believe?" asked Dad.

Ginna was looking earnestly at him. "Yes, it is. In The Book it says, 'All of us have become like one who is unclean, and all our righteous acts are like filthy rags.' Not just the bad things we do, but even the good things we try to do. To the Lord they're still impure and polluted."

As I was nodding, I saw she'd reached over and taken Dad's other hand in hers.

"Gosh, that's really depressing. It seems there's no hope for us at all," he sighed.

"Yes," I heard Celestia add. "And a verse that always seems to haunt me is in *Romans*, chapter three: 'For all have sinned and fall short of the glory of God'."

"But there *is* hope," said Mom quickly. "God promised it through his son. It says in another part of The Book, 'Come now, and let us reason together, says the Lord; though your sins are like scarlet, they shall be as white as snow.' He hasn't given up on us yet."

Now we heard Darroch clear his throat. "I've seen

that, too. This is the reason the Believers were the ones who couldn't accept Tarshiesh's new religion. As a result, they were persecuted and driven from place to place. Many cities and lands were laid waste, as the War of Unification raged on for several years."

I was trying to tell by his voice whether he was a Believer or not, but he remained enigmatic. At last, I just came out and asked him:

"So Darroch, what do you believe?"

"I'm a Believer now," he smiled. "At first, we of the fractured world were just thankful Tarshiesh brought peace and set up a stable government. Most felt his new religion was the right thing—to be open and tolerant of everyone and their individual beliefs. But it turned out this wasn't what Tarshiesh meant, after all. As time went on, his religion became a cult worshipping him alone. To acknowledge any other god became a crime."

"And so the Morotani, the Believers, and many other religious groups began to question Tarshiesh and his system, didn't they?" said Mom.

"System! That sounds just like something in Celestia's time." I blurted this out before I realized what I'd done.

Darroch was looking at me curiously, but Mom jumped back in to divert his attention, "Was this what you call the War of Unification?"

"Uh—yes," he nodded. "As I said, it was a time of terrible suffering and destruction."

"How did it end?" I asked.

"The True King came to Earth and overthrew Tarshiesh. Now we live in his Great Peace."

"The True Lord of Heaven and Earth? My parents talked about him ruling here on Earth, but when they got here, they couldn't find him."

"But Celestia, he's reigning now, even as we speak. When did your parents come here—and from where?"

I could tell he'd caught my comment about 'her time' and knew there was no choice but to tell him the truth, even if he would never believe it.

While I was still trying to decide where to start, Dad spoke up. "Darroch, you mentioned showing us some of the city's sights. Could we do that while the day is still somewhat warm?"

He stood slowly. "Yes, I guess we can still talk while we walk." He was staring at me as he said this, and I knew he wasn't going to let me off the hook.

Soon we were walking away from the Capitol, back toward the Temple Square we'd seen yesterday. This time, though, we stopped in the middle of a large open field, beside the temple building. It was grassy and a few small trees were scattered randomly across it.

"What's this?" Celestia asked.

"This is where the concert hall used to be," said Darroch.

"The what?"

"It existed in my time, Dad," I said.

"What happened to it?" asked Mom.

"When the Morotani rebelled against Tarshiesh, he attacked this city," Darroch went on. "He said he'd destroy all the sacred buildings, including the Temple."

"But the Temple's still here. How did it survive?"

"It was a compromise, I guess you'd call it."

"After the concert hall was razed, the Elders agreed to meet with Tarshiesh and promised they'd follow his religion if he spared the Temple, but he himself must never set foot inside.

"For some reason, Tarshiesh agreed, on the condition that no one else be permitted inside the Temple, except Morotani followers. So it was agreed. That's why you weren't allowed in yesterday," Darroch concluded.

"But if the True King is reigning now, why don't they follow him?"

"I used to be one of the Morotani," Darroch said, with only a slight hesitation in his voice. "Some of us wanted to acknowledge the True King, along with the other Believers. But our Elders had become so drawn in upon themselves they refused to acknowledge anyone else. So, I left the Morotani and became a Believer, but it meant I was cut off from the rest of my family, my heritage."

I found myself looking at my companions as he said this. Each of us knew this experience of feeling cut off—being alone—in our own way.

"I know what that feels like," Celestia sighed softly.

Darroch was staring at her now. "There are some things I'd like to ask you, Celestia, about 'your time'."

"My what?"

"You know what I mean." There was just the slightest smile twitching at his lips.

"Gosh, I'm hungry!" I tried to change the subject. "Hadn't we better head back to the 'Y'? I don't want to miss the main meal of the day."

"Not so fast!" Darroch grinned. "Why don't you all come to my place?"

"Oh, that's a lot of mouths for you to feed," said Mom, trying to come to our rescue.

"It's no problem. Now that the world has peace, we have plenty to share. I insist."

"Thanks for the offer," said Dad. "Is it far to your place?"

"Only a few blocks from here, actually. We can walk."

And so, we set off toward his flat.

***

Darroch served noodles with a red sauce, along with vegetable salad. It was delicious and gave us an excuse not to talk. At last, however, we all cleaned our plates. He was looking at Celestia expectantly, and I knew we had no choice now but to reveal our secret.

"Okay, Darroch," she sighed. "You probably won't believe any of this, and you'll think I'm crazy. But 'my time' is about 900 years in the future."

His eyes widened in surprise, and then he blinked and looked around the table at the others. "Them, too?"

"Oh, nothing is that simple. Garek is from my time, too—the future to you. But Ginna and her daughter are actually from the Twenty-first Century—your past."

Now a deep silence descended on us. I sat looking down at the texture of my empty plate. Eternity seemed to fill the room.

"How did the four of you get together?" he finally asked.

"That's a really complicated story," Mom sighed. "Can we wait on it for awhile?"

"All right, then how did you all get *here*?"

"We were trying to cross the GAP to the Fountain in the Desert—in my own time," Celestia said. "But somehow we fell into a Time Well and ended up here. I'm not very experienced at crossing the GAP. Do you believe any of this, Darroch?"

Now he was smiling at her, which was quite a surprise. "Actually, I do—or rather I want to."

"You do?"

"Well, yes. You see there are a few in my time who've begun to explore this thing you call the GAP—it stands for Galactic Antipaterminal Passage, doesn't it?"

"Yes, how did you know?"

"Like I said, there are a few pioneers in the field. Perhaps you should meet my friend Laken Meta."

"Do you think he could help us?" My heart began to race with hope.

"I have no idea, Annemarie. After all, the science is in its infancy. Celestia may already know more about it than anyone in this century."

"And I don't know all that much. My father does, though. He has some Star Corps training."

"Star Corps?"

"Oh, yeah, I guess that's way off in the future from here. Have people from Earth traveled to any other planets yet?"

"Well, they've sent exploring parties to Mars and to some of the moons of Jupiter. Those trips take years, though. No colonies have been established yet."

"They will be, once the GAP-crossing is perfected," Dad said then.

"It's so amazing that you actually believe us," I added.

He smiled but let his gaze rest the longest on me. I looked down and fidgeted with my hands.

"Garek, you were asking this morning about Tacoma," Darroch turned toward Dad.

"Oh, yeah," Celestia jumped in before he could reply. "We think it may be re-named Tornatoh in our time. It's the only point of reference we have for finding the Fountain we were seeking, when we—uh, first set out."

"Is there a big temple in Tacoma with colored fountains?" Mom asked excitedly.

"I haven't seen one," he sighed. "There was a great earthquake in that area about fifty or sixty years ago. The city just north of it, Seattle, was completely destroyed. Much of the land beneath it fell into the ocean, and the coastline there was changed drastically. But there's been a lot of rebuilding in recent years."

"How can we get there?" Mom asked. "Is there some kind of transportation?"

"There's ground and air transport both," nodded Darroch. "But if you have no money, you have a problem."

"Oh, yeah, all we have is a few credits," Dad said.

Now Darroch rose from his chair and walked excitedly around the room. At a window looking toward the west, he stopped. I slowly rose and joined him. On the horizon, the sun was dipping toward the glimmer of the Great Salt Lake, which was tinged with orange—the way we'd first seen it.

"I have a couple weeks' vacation coming," he said. I could sense him moving slightly closer to me and tried to keep myself from stepping away. "It would be interesting for you to see the revived city of Tacoma. And I do have a groundcar. It would be tight for five people, but it could be done, if you'd like to make the trip with me."

As he said this, he reached over and took my hand. There was a sudden rush of warmth flowing up my arm and into my belly. I hadn't felt this since my lover, James, had held me—a long time ago now.

CHAPTER 7
WORKING OUR WAY WEST

Darroch's groundcar was a tight fit, but we managed by putting Dad in the front seat. There was no way he could fit in the back, with his height and long legs. Mom, Celestia, and I managed to squeeze ourselves into the back seat.

As we left the city, the terrain made a dramatic change. All the land west of the city was a vast plain covered with white sand, blinding in the sunlight.

"All of this used to be part of the Great Salt Lake," Darroch explained. "Over the centuries, it's been evaporating away and shrinking in size. There was a grand old resort hotel on its shores about two hundred years ago."

"That would be around the 1920's," Mom put in. "That's even before my time."

Darroch nodded. I was still wondering if he really believed our story about time-travel. "Anyway," he went on, "It was left high and dry by the mid-Twentieth Century, and now it's been torn down for a long time."

"This whole lake is gone in my time," said Dad, turning to look at Darroch.

I couldn't see Darroch's face, since I was seated right behind him, so I wondered if Dad was able to read anything from what he saw.

"How far is it to Tacoma?" asked Celestia.

"Oh, about 1300 kilometers," Darroch replied.

Mom was the only one who didn't seem surprised at this. The rest of us tried not to moan at the thought of being crammed into this groundcar for so long.

"How long will that take us, at your best ground-speed?" Dad said, finally.

"Well, usually I can make it in two days' drive," he replied. "Since this country is so remote, I have to use a wheeled groundcar. They have a longer range than a hover-car, and there aren't many charging stations here in the desert. I'm sorry if it's uncomfortable for all of you—hovercars are roomier. I know you'll want to stop and stretch your legs. We'll just see how far we get this first day."

"Do you travel to Tacoma often?" I asked.

"I have relatives there, so maybe once a year."

Then we all settled into silence. Gradually, off in the distance, some foothills began to emerge from the haze. The sun shining on us through the car's glassed sides began to feel hot, and I tried not to think about the discomfort. Despite my desire to look at the scene around us, I closed my eyes, just to keep the brightness out until the sun set.

***

I must have dozed off and slept most of the night, for the next thing I knew we were stopped near the top of a ridge, and the sun was rising behind us. The others were just climbing out, stretching tired legs and backs, so I joined them.

"Where are we?" I heard Celestia ask.

"Finally made it halfway across Idaho," said Darroch.

"Ah, yes, that was the state just north of Utah," she nodded. "I think my parents lived somewhere up this way, when my mother was working in Salien."

I glanced at Dad as she referred to Salien, but I couldn't tell what his reaction was.

"This area looks very bleak," I sighed. "All we can see is this rough black rock, and those humpy-looking ridges."

"Part of this area used to be called 'Craters of the Moon'," said Dad. "People thought it looked like the surface of the moon."

Darroch looked sidelong at him, seeming surprised he knew so much about the area, if it really was so long before his time. Again, I wondered if he was doubting our story.

"Well, about sixty years ago, the Yellowstone Caldera erupted and spewed ash and lava for hundreds of miles around," Darroch said. "Now the 'Craters of the Moon' probably can describe an area many times larger than it originally did."

"Yes," nodded Dad. "It was named in the Twentieth Century, I believe. Old records at the Forestry Commission say that back then Yellowstone was a lush pine-forested area, full of many kinds of wildlife, hot springs, and geysers."

"What are geysers?" Celestia asked, looking confused.

"They're groundwater heated by molten rock in the earth below. Sometimes, when super-heated, they spout up like steaming, hot fountains."

"Could one of those be the Fountain we're looking for?" I asked.

"I doubt it," Darroch shrugged. "Almost all of the geysers were destroyed or greatly altered when the volcano beneath the whole area finally erupted. Yellowstone as it was no longer exists."

"How sad," I heard Mom say. "It was a popular place for tourists in my time, and I always wanted to see it. Now I guess I never will."

"Maybe you'll get back to your own time someday," said Dad, and I saw him reach for her hand. Again, she didn't pull away, and I smiled.

While they were talking, a loud screeching sound filled my ears. Looking up, I saw a strange red-colored bird flying past. It was moving so fast that it disappeared before I could say a word. Wondering what it was, I moved to where Celestia was scanning the horizon and knew she was trying to compare it to descriptions her parents had given of the desert where they found the Fountain.

"They mentioned a lone, red cliff jutting up from the desert floor," she told me. "But there's nothing like that here. All the rock around us is black."

"Some seems to still show signs of how it flowed when it was molten," I said and pointed this out to Darroch.

He smiled. "That ropy-looking rock was super-hot and flowed quickly before it cooled."

"What about the blocky, broken stuff?"

"That lava cooled faster on top, Annemarie. Then it cracked as the hotter molten lava kept flowing underneath it."

As he was talking, he pointed to examples around us. Then he casually rested his arm around my waist, and I felt a warm tingle again.

"Well, if you all are ready, I think we should press on," he said, at last.

Once again, we squeezed into the groundcar. I tried to keep my mind occupied by watching the scenery change.

"Did you see that red bird, Celestia?" I whispered after we'd gone a little way. But she shook her head, and I was left to wonder.

After a couple of hours, there finally began to be breaks in the vast blackness of solidified lava. Most of these were ridges of lighter-colored rock which probably were high peaks before the lava flows.

Now they were like islands standing above the black sea of rock. Off in the distance were three cone-shaped peaks I thought must be volcanoes. I wondered if they were still active.

I mentioned this to Mom, who was seated next to me. "Yes, in our time there were several volcanoes people thought were extinct."

"Like Mount St. Helen's?" I asked.

"The Yellowstone one, too," added Dad from the front seat.

"Have there been a lot of volcanic eruptions and earthquakes in the past century, Darroch?" Mom asked.

"I've heard there are many more in the Twenty-second Century than there were in the previous two hundred years," he said.

Silence settled then, but a few minutes later Mom added, "You know, all this reminds me of a place in The Book talking about signs of the end."

"The end?" Dad asked.

"When the King returns to rule?" I added.

"Yes, in the book called *Matthew* he says, 'Nation will rise against nation, and kingdom against kingdom. There will be famines and earthquakes in various places. All these are the beginning of birth pains'."

"That's in The Book?"

Mom nodded.

"This Book is our Bible, right Ginna?" said Darroch.

"Yes."

"Well, it all fits then." He turned slightly and I could see him smile. "We had nearly a century of all those things.

But now, at last, the birth is beginning, for the King has come."

"That's great," I heard Dad say.

I glanced at Mom, and saw she had the same question in her eyes that was in my mind: 'If the King is reigning now, why are Believers being persecuted in future times?' I shrugged to her, hoping we'd find an answer to this paradox.

A couple of hours later, we came to a small hamlet alongside the road, and stopped again for a stretch break. Darroch went inside a store nearby, but when he came out he was shaking his head. "They don't know of any lodging places here anymore. They've all been closed down."

I've forgotten to mention our road was merely a two-lane strip of blacktop, which matched the lava beds around us. It looked like it was built after lava flowed here, meaning it was fairly new.

"What happened to all the fields and highways and towns that were here before?" Mom asked, echoing my thoughts.

"They were all buried under many feet of lava and ash," sighed Darroch. "This used to be a fertile farming valley, with a river flowing through a deep canyon. But everything changed with the Yellowstone Eruption. Now it's pretty desolate."

"So where are we going to stay the night?" Dad asked.

"Actually, I thought we'd try driving through the night

again, if you all are willing. It won't be nearly as hot, so it'll be easier on the car."

"Maybe not easier on my backside!" Dad laughed his explosive laugh. "How are you women doing back there?"

"Oh, I guess we'll manage," I sighed, as we climbed into the car once again.

Actually, I wanted to get to Tacoma as soon as possible anyway, hoping we might find answers to some of our questions there.

***

Again, I dozed through most of the night. Once in awhile, I'd wake and see the sides of the road sliding by in the dark. Toward the end of the night, I saw the moon as it made its way west. By its angle off to my left, I could tell we were traveling in a northwesterly direction. There seemed to be a high ridge of peaks between us and the western horizon, looming ominously in the dark.

Gradually dawn sent fingers of light onto these peaks, and I began to make out some of their shapes. A few looked vaguely familiar to me. Just as the sun rose above the eastern horizon, our road turned west and began winding its way into the foothills. As we approached the mountain range, I could see a canyon coming into view. The road followed this, as it wound its way up toward a pass to the other side of the range.

"What are these mountains called?" I asked, at last, though I had a feeling I knew.

"These are the Cascades," said Darroch.

"I wonder if these have been renamed 'Cruax' in my time," said Celestia, stifling a yawn. "That was the name of the mountains my parents crossed on their way to the Fountain."

"How much farther?" I asked, but now that I knew my guess about the Cascades was right, I was wondering how far we were from my old home in Portland—and how much it had changed in the past century.

"We'll see the lights of the city soon," he replied.

"Really? I thought you said it would take two days."

"Well, you all were sleeping so well, and I felt fine, so I just kept on driving. I've made this trip in one long haul before," Darroch smiled. "There, see those lights down there. Those are the outskirts of Tacoma."

Sure enough, we could see the lines of lights marking roads, just as we'd seen in Salt Lake City when we descended from the mountains east of it. This city was much larger, however, for the lights seemed to stretch as far as my eyes could see.

"It's huge," I cried, and saw Darroch turn to smile at me.

"Don't worry, you won't have to stay at the 'Y' here," he laughed. "We'll go to my friend Laken's place."

I remembered he'd mentioned this name when we were telling him about our Time Well. Hadn't he said his friend knew something about crossing the GAP?

Soon, we dropped down the last long hill and emerged onto the level valley where the city lay. Now the lights, which appeared to be tiny pinpricks, revealed themselves to be signs, streetlamps, and windows of many tall buildings. Darroch maneuvered his groundcar through the maze of streets, seeming to know exactly where he was going.

"Did you say you have relatives here?" I asked.

"Yes. But I prefer to stay at my friend's place. My aunt and uncle have a very small flat, and all five of us would overwhelm them," he laughed.

It appeared we were approaching the center of the city, if the increasing height of the buildings was any indication. Just as he pulled the car into a tall parking garage and found a place to park, the sun finally sent light into the canyons between the buildings. But it was still dark inside the garage when he turned off the groundcar's lights. A few overhead lamps gave a little light, and a sign pointed the way to a lift.

Once we were inside the lift, I saw him take out a pocket-com and press a number. "Hey, Laken! Good morning, it's Darroch. Better get dressed. I'm coming up with a big surprise for you."

He listened for a few seconds to the reply I couldn't hear. "No, I'm not joking. You won't believe what stumbled into my life. But you'll find it fascinating, I guarantee. We're in the lift right now, so you'd better get ready to buzz us in."

"Are you sure we won't be bothering him?" I asked quickly.

He grinned at me, and then at the rest of us. "Oh, no. He'll be delighted to meet all of you."

CHAPTER 8
LAKEN OF TACOMA

We were seated in an airy room, with large windows overlooking the city and furnishings in various shades of brown and green.

"Is this real leather upholstery?" I asked.

Mom glanced sharply at me. I guess she thought I was being impolite, but Laken only smiled and nodded.

"I like old things. My place is sort of a tribute to your time, I guess you could say."

I turned in surprise when he said 'your time.' Perhaps he believed our time-travel story, too.

When we'd arrived that morning, Laken greeted us at his door with great curiosity on his face. He was in many ways the opposite of his friend Darroch. His hair was also black, but straight and long, pulled back in a ponytail that hung down his back. His eyes were dark, too, but more of a soft brown with a slight slant. His skin was a warm shade of brown, and he seemed quieter and more reserved than Darroch.

"So, what is this great surprise, my friend?" was the first thing he said. "I haven't seen you in months, and now you turn up out of the blue with four people."

Darroch told him our story with some assistance from us, and I watched as Laken's eyes grew wider in surprise at each new revelation. "You mean in the future people actually cross the GAP to navigate the Galaxy?" he asked.

"Yes, but we must be interfaced with a starship," Celestia nodded. "We can also move instantaneously on planetary surfaces if we have the coordinates."

"But what about this time-travel?" Laken couldn't hide the excitement in his voice.

"My father, Jon, was one who experimented with it a lot," Celestia continued, "And my Uncle Jael, my mother's younger brother—he and Dad had some sort of special connection."

"You actually time-traveled to get here?" asked Laken.

"Not exactly," she sighed. "We were trying to travel across Earth, in the Thirty-first Century."

"The what?"

"Yes, you heard me correctly. We fell into a Time Well, and came back over 900 years."

"That's like a wormhole but on a planetary surface," Mom added.

Laken kept on asking questions, many of which we couldn't answer. Then he suddenly seemed to realize we might be hungry after our long trip, and offered to fix some breakfast.

Along with a delicious omelet, he served us some good coffee. This was something I hadn't experienced in a long time.

Now we were sitting in his comfortable leather chairs and looking out at the city of Tacoma. In the distance, we could see the shores of the Pacific Ocean.

"There used to be a big bay out there called Puget Sound," Darroch was saying, "But the whole coastline changed in the Great Seattle Earthquake."

"And that was how long ago?" asked Dad.

"Almost sixty years now. We're finally getting back to some semblance of normalcy," Laken smiled.

Mom rose from her seat and was studying some pictures hanging on the wall. Then she pointed to one and let out a little cry of surprise, "Isn't this the Space Needle?"

Laken rose to join her. "Yes. Beautiful, isn't it? Too bad it was lost in the earthquake, along with most of the rest of Seattle."

"Could this be the tower Martina and the others told us about seeing in Tornatoh?" she asked, turning to the rest of us.

"That doesn't make sense," I said. "If it was destroyed sixty years ago, how could it still exist in the future?"

"Maybe they'll rebuild it. Do you think they might?" She turned to Laken, but he shrugged:

"Haven't heard of any plans to."

By now, I was looking closely at the picture, too, with

my hand on Mom's shoulder. She closed her eyes and seemed to concentrate her vision inward. I wondered if she was trying to access some of Martina's memories from Tornatoh—or perhaps even Terres.

"They said the tower in Tornatoh looked like Neptune Spire," she said softly.

"What's that?" Laken asked.

"It was the symbol of the Galactic System, and every System Planet had one. But I don't remember it having those tripod base supports. It seemed like just one huge cylinder rising hundreds of feet into the air. There was a disc shape at the top, but it was taller and not as wide as this one, in proportion to the tower. Also, there was a tall, needle-like spire on the top."

Laken suddenly clapped his hands and went to a desk in the corner of the room. After rummaging in a couple of drawers, he pulled out another picture. "I used to have this one on the wall, too," he said. "This was called the CN Tower. I think they changed the name to Unity Tower, and it's in Toronto, which is now the capital of the United World State of Ontario.

He handed the picture to Mom and I saw her face light up. "Yes, that's the image I see in Martina's memories."

"You see it where?" Laken looked at her suspiciously.

"Oh, it's too complicated to explain right now," Celestia cut in quickly. I could tell she wasn't ready to reveal any more of her father's secrets about time-travel and parallel universes to these strangers. We'd probably told them too much already. "I've seen the Tornatoh tower, too. This is exactly what it looks like," she said then.

'She isn't really lying,' I told myself. 'We did see a quick glimpse of it when we went there in search of Dad.'

"Hmm," I heard Darroch speak for the first time in awhile. "I can see Toronto's name getting shifted to 'Tornatoh' over time, can't you, Laken?"

His friend nodded and their eyes met. "But I haven't heard of a range of tall mountains and a desert to the east of Toronto, like your friends describe."

"Perhaps there will be many geological and climate changes during the next 900 years," said Dad.

"That's probably true," added Mom.

"We've already seen some climate changes, even just in my lifetime," nodded Laken. "The polar icecaps are shrinking almost to nothing, glaciers are disappearing all over the world, and the coastlines have been altered by sea level rise and tsunamis—not to mention the earthquakes all around the Pacific Rim. It seems like the faults there have become more active."

"Yes." Darroch moved over to the window. "My uncle always talks about how different his view of the ocean is from when he was a boy."

Just then, as if by some terrible coincidence, the floor beneath my feet began to tremble. Then things were shaking off the wall and sliding off tables onto the floor.

"Earthquake!" cried Laken. "We still get them often. Quick, find a spot under the dining table."

Soon we were all huddled there as the room continued to shudder and sway.

"Now I know why you like this sturdy old furniture!" Darroch shouted, to be heard above the rumbling all around us.

I'd never experienced anything like this, and just put my hands over my head, burying it between my knees.

When at last the shuddering and trembling stopped, and I could feel my own heartbeat again, I slowly lifted my head. "Does this happen often?" I asked in a shaky voice.

"Not every day—or even every month," Laken tried to smile. "But enough that I've felt a few. This one is the strongest one so far."

I nodded, and then suddenly realized Darroch had his arm around my shoulders, holding me tightly. I couldn't tell who was more frightened—him or me. Glancing across from me, I saw Mom hugging Dad for dear life. Celestia was the only one sitting alone, but she just shrugged when Laken moved to take her hand. Then he stood up, and began to push debris out of the way, so we could crawl out from under the table.

"Oh, Laken, all your beautiful pictures," said Celestia.

"I can get new frames," he smiled. "And it looks like most of the photographs themselves are all right."

We tried the best we could to clean up Laken's flat, but a couple of the windows had broken in the quake, too. "I'm afraid we can't sleep here tonight," he sighed. "The night air will be too cold."

"We're used to sleeping outdoors," I said. "As long as you have an extra blanket or two, we should be fine."

"I'm not sure we should stay indoors at all," Laken added. "There may be aftershocks, especially after such a powerful quake."

Darroch nodded. "Right, I should've thought of that. I wonder where we can go."

"I'd suggest an open area, like a city square or a park," said Laken.

"Boy, I wish we could just cross a GAP to another place," I said to Celestia. "We didn't realize how easy we had it—or rather will have it—in the future."

Laken was looking at her closely now. "You really do know how to do a GAP-crossing, don't you?" I was beginning to see his interest in Celestia was both personal and scientific, and perhaps Darroch was encouraging this by increasing his attentions to me.

"I've crossed to Tornatoh before. If I had coordinates I could do it now."

"Do you remember the ones we used when we crossed from Darien's compound?" I asked.

"I might recognize them if I saw them. But that was starting from a different place than here in Tacoma."

"And in a different time, too," added Mom.

Just then the floor began to shake again. "Oh, no!" I cried.

"Aftershock!" shouted Laken.

Fortunately, this was a small one, for soon the trembling stopped. "I think we'd better pack up what we can carry and look for an outdoor place to camp," said Darroch.

Without speaking, Laken began pulling things out of the piles of stuff fallen from the cabinets and tables. "Here's some food that should travel fairly well. And take just one change of clothes for each of us."

Fortunately, we'd brought our packsacks up when we'd parked Darroch's car. As we crammed stuff into them, I suddenly thought of the groundcar:

"Would it help if we found your car, Darroch?"

"It's probably crushed by the upper levels of the parking garage by now," he sighed. "It would be dangerous to go in there. Besides, the roads are most likely too damaged to be drivable."

"Oh, I hadn't thought of that."

"Say, Laken, do you have any maps here?" Dad suddenly asked.

"Luckily, I did have a drawerful of antique paper maps in my desk. Oh here, some of them are on the floor now." He grabbed any he could see and stuffed them into his pack. "I guess they might come in handy."

Just as we were going through the door, another aftershock began. "Head for the stairs," called Laken. "The elevators are shut down for sure."

Racing down the tilting and shifting stairs, we tried to keep our balance. It seemed we were running for ages and would never reach the bottom. But just as the shaking stopped again, we came to a place where the steps ended with a drop of at least a meter. We jumped down to a large door that was wedged open only about ten centimeters.

The men were pushing on it, but it didn't budge. So Celestia and I joined in to help. At last, it shifted about twenty centimeters further open.

"There must be debris blocking it," Laken shouted. "Let me see if I can squeeze out and move some of it. I think I'm the smallest one here."

He did have a very slim build and slipped through the opening easily. Before anyone else spoke, I worked my way through the narrow space and was out of the building right behind him.

A shocking sight met my eyes, and I could do nothing but stare for a few moments. Darroch was right about the roads being impassible. In fact, the debris was so deep and chaotic it was hard to tell what had been streets and what had been buildings.

"My God!" Laken muttered. "How did we even survive this?"

"We should thank God we did," I whispered almost to myself.

"Yeah, I guess so. Come on, we need to try to move some of this rubble, so the door can open just a bit wider."

There were bricks and heavy slabs of concrete, but we managed to shift them just enough to get the door opened a few centimeters more. Darroch, Celestia, and Mom managed to wriggle out, but it was still too tight a fit for Dad, so we all heaved together to get one last piece of concrete out of the door's path.

"Whew, I guess I *do* need to lose weight," he chuckled softly when he'd finally squeezed through the narrow opening.

I saw Mom smile up at him and pat his back.

None of us spoke for awhile after that, but just tried to pick our way in whatever direction seemed easiest. There was no way to really get our bearings, and Laken was the only one who really knew the layout of the city—or what it had been.

Sometimes we seemed to be going in circles, and I could see the sun beginning to sink into the west. Before long, it would be dark, and we still didn't know where we were, or if there was any place safe from more falling debris.

At last, we all plopped onto what appeared to be the remains of some stone steps. "I can't go on," sighed Mom. "My head is spinning."

"Here, drink some water," offered Dad. "I should've been paying more attention. You're probably getting dehydrated."

"I can't even tell where we are, and this is my hometown," sighed Laken.

"Yeah, I thought I'd been here enough to find *something* I'd recognize," added Darroch.

"Let's take a look at one of those maps," Dad pointed to Laken's pack.

"Go ahead. I'm not even sure which ones I grabbed, or if they'll be any help. But have at it."

As we sat, Dad started to shuffle through the maps. He seemed to be looking for something in particular, not just browsing through them. Moving closer to him, Celestia and I began to look over his shoulder.

Most of the maps didn't look at all familiar to me, until he pulled one out which depicted a much larger area than the others. There was a continent labeled 'North America'.

"That's where I lived," I cried, pointing to the western section, where Colorado would be.

"I've heard of this," Celestia said, looking near my finger. "North America was an old name for the area my family lived in."

"That's right," Dad smiled. Then he pointed to some very large lakes. "There are the so-called Great Lakes, see? And here's Toronto."

I looked at the city he indicated. It was lying along the north shore of the lake labeled Ontario.

"Didn't Laken say Toronto was the capital of the State of Ontario?" I asked, "And that there was a tower there?"

"Yes, I did. Is it on one of my maps?" Laken leaned closer to examine the map in Dad's hands.

"Sure is," nodded Dad. "And look what else I found." He was pointing to numbers written along the top, sides, and bottom of the map.

"What are those?"

"Latitude and longitude numbers, Celestia. I'm hoping these are the original basis of the coordinates you use."

We both stared at them and I could tell she was trying to embed them in her mind—*43 degrees, 38 seconds North; 79 degrees, 30 minutes West*—but I couldn't tell if they were the same coordinates we'd used before.

"Coordinates?" cried Mom. "You mean we might be able to get there?"

"I have no idea," said Dad. "I'm new at all this. Celestia knows more about it than all the rest of us combined, I think."

"And that's not much," she sighed. "Laken, do you know anything about crossing the GAP?"

I turned to find his brown eyes boring into Celestia's. "It's all theoretical at this point. The facts indicate there should be a way to manipulate space through this fifth dimension, but all I know is the mathematical formulae."

As he was saying this, we suddenly began to hear shouts not far from us. "Stop!" cried a voice. "Please, don't hurt us!"

"What is it?" I cried.

"I think looters are coming out with the night," whispered Laken. "We need to get out of sight."

"But shouldn't we try to help?" asked Celestia.

"There's nothing we can do right now." Laken's voice sounded very tense. "We have no weapons. Just follow me, and don't say a word."

He jumped up then, and we all followed as he worked his way deeper into a pile of debris. Soon we were crouched as close to the ground as we could, peering out into the darkening twilight. Out of sight, we could hear the sounds of running feet and then a blood-curdling scream. Loud bangs like gunshots rang out and seemed to be coming closer.

"What should we do?" I hissed in someone's ear. I wasn't sure which of the men was next to me.

"Sh!" came Darroch's tense whisper. "They're trying to flush us out like a hawk harrying a mouse."

The sounds were getting much too close for me. Suddenly, I heard Celestia whisper to me, "Get everyone's hands joined." I passed this on to Darroch, and he nodded. Then I felt another hand join my left one, and I concentrated every ounce of my being with Celestia's—on those latitude and longitude numbers we'd seen for Toronto.

CHAPTER 9
THE CITY ON THE LAKE

The next thing I felt was cold water washing over my feet and splashing around my knees.

"Where *are* we?" It was a male voice I heard, but I couldn't tell whose.

"Darroch, where are *you*?" Now I recognized Laken's voice.

"I'm right here on your left."

Gradually, I realized the fog before my eyes was real, and not an effect from crossing the GAP. Hopefully, this was a good sign—maybe we'd crossed successfully.

"Keep hold of each other's hands," came Celestia's voice. "Just step forward one step."

As I'd hoped, faces came into focus through the white haze. "Step again now," she called.

Finally, I could see all six of us. "I think we're on the edge of a lake," Celestia added. "Maybe even Lake Ontario. Can anyone tell which way the shore is?"

"It seemed shallower behind me," came Mom's voice.

"Okay, move toward Ginna," she said.

Soon the water did get shallower, and when we finally reached dry sand, we all let go of each other's hands, as if on cue.

A low moaning sound reached my ears. Yes, a foghorn. At least we knew we were on shore now, but what shore?

"Where are we, Celestia?" I could tell Laken was already excited about where he thought we might be.

Then I felt Darroch take my hand again and begin to pull me along with him. "Let's try to get further inland. Maybe the fog will be thinner, and we can get some points of reference."

Sure enough, as we walked, the land began to rise. Clambering through the loose sand, we climbed over a dune. Once on the other side, the fog was indeed thinning. After we'd walked several meters further, I began to make out the shapes of tall buildings looming out of the mist.

"Look!" cried Celestia. "It's a city."

"And it's not Tacoma." Now I knew Laken guessed what we'd done. He walked up to Celestia and put both his hands on her shoulders. "How did you do that?"

"Cross the GAP?"

"Just like that—you can do it?" His voice was full of disbelief.

"What are you two talking about?" Now Darroch stepped up beside him.

"There's something vaguely familiar about this city," Mom was saying, as she also stepped toward me.

"I think it looks similar to Tornatoh," Dad said.

"It should, if Toronto and Tornatoh are the same city in two different times." Celestia's voice was getting more excited.

"You did cross the GAP, didn't you?" Darroch suddenly shouted. "Do you know what this means, Laken?"

Laken was nodding. "This is the proof I hoped for, that it could be done. But it seemed so instantaneous. I didn't feel a thing. First, we were hiding in the rubble, and then we were standing in the lake."

"Fortunately, the coordinates I used didn't put us in the *middle* of Lake Ontario."

"How did you find coordinates, Celestia? I didn't think there was any way to get them in this century," said Mom.

"I used those latitude and longitude numbers Garek found. Apparently, they were close enough to get us here."

"But how does it work?" Laken was beginning to make me uncomfortable with the way he kept looking at us and asking these prodding questions.

Finally, Celestia turned and looked him in the eye. "To be honest, I don't know all the details, Laken. It's a power that only first-born can develop. Are you first-born?"

"Uh—yes."

"Well, then perhaps you'll begin to sense it and learn."

"But how?"

"In my time, people are trained at the Star Corps Academies. My father was, for a time. He's the one who taught me, because I didn't have any opportunity to attend an Academy."

I hoped this explanation would satisfy him, for I knew Celestia didn't really want to go into all the details about what the future held—the development of the System and their erasure of Earth from the history and memory of humans. It was too complicated to explain, and something in my mind told me it wasn't a good idea to reveal the future to people this far back in the past.

By this time, all of us were slowly walking across the remainder of the beach toward a grassy park. Just on the other side of this was a wide street. Many kinds of vehicles were moving up and down it, some hovercraft and some with wheels. There were also small aircraft buzzing overhead.

As I was about to wonder how we could ever get across this thoroughfare, Darroch pointed to a tunnel entrance nearby. "I think that will take us under the street to the city."

The inside of the tunnel was well-lit, with gleaming white walls. There were even little kiosks and shops spreading out to either side. This reminded me that at least four of us couldn't purchase anything in this time, and my stomach growled at the thought.

At the end of the tunnel, we stepped onto a moving set of stairs.

"They called this an escalator in my time," said Mom.

"We do, too," nodded Laken.

I felt unsteady as I stepped on the moving stairs. Even though I'd been on one before, I never seemed to get used to them, so I clung to the hand rail.

"If there were any of these in my parents' youth on Terres, they never mentioned it," Celestia whispered to me, as she shakily stepped onto the escalator. "I've never seen one, but then I spent most of my life in the mountains and the wilds."

As we emerged into the city, it felt like we were in a deep canyon, except the walls were buildings, some so tall their tops were shrouded in the fog. Most had many lighted windows looking down on us like staring eyes. It reminded me of my recent view of snowy Denver, just before Celestia came to me—and I shuddered. Then I saw her gazing upward, seeming awestruck by the size of everything.

"You haven't seen many cities, have you?" Darroch slipped up beside me while I was staring upward with her.

"What should we do now?" I asked. I didn't feel like answering his questions about my personal life.

"Hey, I thought *you two* had an idea," he said, looking over at Celestia.

"I was just trying to get away from those looters," she sighed, "And this was the only place I could cross to…"

"Oh my gosh!"

"What, Mom?"

"Look at the tower—there it is," she was pointing to a large cylindrical building directly across the street from us, rising high into the sky with its top hidden in the fog.

"You mean that's the tower you saw in Tornatoh?" I asked. "We can't even see the top, so how can you tell?"

"I just know by how the base looks and how it feels," Mom shrugged. "Why don't we walk around and see if anything else looks familiar to me—or you and Celestia. We're the only ones here who've been to Tornatoh."

"Hey, what about me? I lived there for a little while, you know."

"Oh Garek, I forgot," she sighed. "Of course. You probably have the best chance of recognizing something."

"Hopefully I will," he said. "I agree with Ginna. It does look like the Tornatoh Tower. But I think we should try to find something to eat first. I can't think too well on an empty stomach."

"I was thinking about that," I sighed. "But we don't have any of the money or credits—or whatever they use here."

"Don't worry. Laken and I will take care of it." Darroch put his arm around me and pulled me close as he spoke. I wasn't sure how I felt about this and wondered if he'd expect some sort of payback for his kindness.

***

After walking up and down several streets, we found a small café on a side street which looked fairly private. We knew, with the things we needed to discuss, it would be better to have few listening ears around.

Once we ordered some food Laken and Darroch recommended, Celestia and I excused ourselves to the restroom.

As soon as we knew no one else was in there, I stepped close where I could whisper to her. "Do you feel like I do—that something is a little off here?"

She nodded. "If the True King is ruling Earth, why were there people in Salt Lake City who wanted to rob us, and why did the looters in Tacoma come out after the earthquake?"

"Why are there still earthquakes and disasters at all? I thought the Heaven and Earth were supposed to be renewed and perfect when the King came. But maybe that's not until later—after your time, Celestia."

"Well, that's true, Annemarie. We aren't in paradise in my time either. I need to get a copy of The Book and see what it says about the time of the King's return," she said. "It seems to me there was something about a thousand years, but it was always confusing to me."

"Maybe they have one of those libraries here, like we saw in Salt Lake City."

"Of course. I'm sure they'd have a copy of The Book—uh, I mean the Bible. That's what they call it now, isn't it?"

"Come on, Celestia, we'd better get back before anyone thinks we got lost."

When we rejoined the rest, the food had arrived. This time I found myself eating something familiar—fried eggs with toasted bread and some smoked ham.

"This is very different from what I eat back home," said Celestia. "We rarely fry eggs over our cooking fire, but we do smoke meat when we can get it."

"You keep sounding like you're camping all the time," said Darroch, eyeing her strangely.

"Oh, it *is* something we like to do, when we *can*." As she glanced at me, I knew she realized her life in the wilds was not at all what they expected the distant future to be like. We must be more careful what we said.

Once breakfast was eaten and paid for, we gathered our packs and set out, trying to look like tourists come to see the city.

As we walked, Mom said, "You know, if that temple is built yet, it should be near the lakeshore."

"That's right. My parents said there were a bunch of stalls selling 'holy water' along Lake Street," Celestia added.

Carefully watching street signs, we tried to see if anything looked familiar. Most of the streets seemed to have strange names, like 'Bloor' and 'Edlington'. Then we came to a wide boulevard running from the lake toward the north, with the name Younge Street.

"This one seems to go a long way."

"Yes," nodded Dad. "It runs from the northern edge of the city all the way down to the city center here. Let's head toward the water. That's where Lake Street should be."

"Do you recognize this Younge Street, then?" Laken asked.

Dad nodded. "It's not the common spelling of the name."

As we worked our way back toward the lake, we crossed a street named 'King', and I wondered if this name was connected with the King they said was reigning over the Earth. When we got back to the thoroughfare running between the city and the shore, it was indeed named 'Lake Street'.

"Boy, how did we miss this before?"

"Well, Annemarie, we used the tunnel last time, and I guess we couldn't see the sign," Darroch smiled at me.

"But there's no temple here yet," sighed Mom.

"And no fountains, either," I added.

"Well, they've got almost nine hundred years to get it built, you know," said Dad.

I realized then I'd expected to move forward in time as we crossed the GAP, but of course we hadn't. The only coordinates we used were physical, latitude and longitude.

"But if this is going to become Tornatoh, then we know the Fountain in the Desert will be somewhere to the east of here, won't it?" said Dad.

"Theoretically," said Mom. "But the desert and the mountains may not even be there yet. It's a long time to that future."

"Perhaps if we got there, to the right place, we could cross into the right time." Darroch was looking at Celestia with questioning eyes, as he said this.

But she shook her head. "How can we find a place that isn't even there yet?" Suddenly she just plopped down on the sidewalk and buried her head in her hands. "I've made a huge mess of this whole thing. I have no idea how to get us out of a Time Well."

Despite her attempts to stop them, tears began to slide down her cheeks. I quickly joined her, putting my arm around her. "Don't blame yourself, Celestia."

"But it *is* my fault. I was supposed to take you to the Fountain, and here we are in the wrong time and the wrong place."

"The Lord must have a reason for allowing this," Mom whispered. "We can't see it now, but maybe someday we will."

Dad sat down next to me, and Darroch moved to my other side, gently running his hands across my back. I hoped he was just trying to comfort me.

"This place isn't all that bad, is it?" he murmured in my ear.

All I could do was shake my head. I really wasn't sure what to say. There was something drawing me to him, but there was doubt lurking in the back of my mind, too. 'Maybe this is what Mom's feeling about Garek? Perhaps there's some natural aversion to being intimate with a person from another time.'

Then I felt a movement beside me and saw my dad draw Mom into his embrace. Well, she seemed to be overcoming her doubts, anyway.

I could sense Darroch wanted to hug me, too, but pushed myself to a standing position before he could. "Okay, you all keep asking us, but now I'm going to ask you, Darroch and Laken, since you're from this time. What should we do now?"

"Well, I suppose we could find the YMCA," Darroch laughed.

"The what?"

"Just a joke, Laken," he said. "I think we can do better than that. There has to be some kind of affordable hotel in this city."

Wearily, we shouldered our packs again and began working our way back toward the city center. After walking for several blocks, past many office and apartment buildings, we finally came to an area with some less modern buildings. One of these had a brick front and concrete steps.

"This looks like something from my time," said Mom. "There's even an old-fashioned neon sign." She pointed to a sign above the door. It wasn't lit now, during the day, but twisted glass tubing formed letters that read 'Comfort Hotel'.

"Let's hope they live up to their name," I said, realizing I couldn't remember how long it was since I'd slept.

Walking through the double glass doors, we entered a large room with plush carpet on the floor. In front of us loomed a dark-colored wooden counter, and a dark-skinned young man smiled up at us. "May I help you?"

"We'd like rooms for tonight," said Laken.

"Would that be three separate rooms?"

Suddenly I saw Laken smile. "Uh, no—we're not actually couples. We'd like two rooms—one for three men and one for three women."

Relief washed over me as I heard him say this. Mom glanced over and gave a grateful smile, too. At least, we wouldn't have to make any decisions about potential relationships yet.

Our hotel room had two beds, each just large enough for two people to sleep in.

"Hey," said Mom, "These look like old-fashioned double beds from my childhood. This place must be really old to still have these. Most hotels have gone to larger beds, even in my time."

"Oh, I've seen some of these, Mom. Guess I've stayed in a lot of old hotels." After I said this, there was an uncomfortable moment of silence, until Celestia spoke:

"Ginna, you take that bed—Annemarie and I can share this one. We're the young ones here."

"All right. I'll take advantage of my old age, for once," she smiled.

"Mom, you're not old."

"I feel old right now—after all that walking and crawling through rubble in Tacoma. Sometimes I wish we had horses, like Splash."

"You mean Uncle Jael's pinto?" said Celestia. "You rode him a lot in the Safe Zone, didn't you?"

Mom nodded. "I guess a horse would be awkward, though. Now that we've traveled so far."

"That's for sure, Mom. We've even crossed a GAP."

"I miss Splash, though," she murmured, "Not to mention Jael and all the others."

As we moved closer to the bed, Celestia changed the subject. "This doesn't look that small to me. Look, it even has two mattresses."

"The top one is the mattress, Celestia," I giggled. "The bottom one is the box-springs."

By this time, she'd seated herself on the bed. "Wow, this is really comfortable. I've never slept on anything like it. Back home all we ever had was a sleeping mat on the floor."

"Well, I'd say this will beat the floor of a cave or a hut," Mom said, lying on her bed with arms and legs spread-eagled, smiling up at the ceiling.

Soon, we were settled in our beds, and before long I could hear Mom snoring softly.

"Annemarie, are you still awake?" Celestia whispered.

"Um-hmm."

"Can I ask you a personal question?"

"Sure."

"What's it like when you make love?" Silence fell for a few minutes, as I tried to think what I should say to her.

"What's it like?" I finally whispered. "Well, sometimes it's absolutely amazing—there's no feeling like it, so how can I describe it? But it has to be with the right person, someone you really love—or it's just disappointing."

"I wonder what it's like for the man."

"That I can't help you with," I snickered.

"I had a boyfriend once, but we never made love," said Celestia.

"Did you love him?"

"I thought I did, as much as I knew about love in my teens. How could I not help loving Patrick?" She seemed to be looking at something faraway. It startled me when I realized the events she was remembering as past actually hadn't happened yet, from where we were now in the Twenty-second Century.

"He and I had so much in common. We both liked to read the same kind of books. And do things outdoors, like hike and ski. He made me feel so warm and comfortable, when he held me in his arms and kissed me. I was crushed when he dumped me, with no explanation at all. I found out later from someone else that he and his old girlfriend had gotten back together. Needless to say, I'm leery of men and their intentions now." She was staring at the ceiling, as though she might find some answers out in the sky somewhere. Then she wiped angrily at her damp cheeks and looked back at me.

"Say, I've noticed Darroch seems to have an attraction to you. How do you feel about that, Annemarie?"

"I've got mixed feelings, and I wonder why. Sometimes I miss my lover James, from the past. But I'm beginning to realize this isn't the way the Lord intends for love to be." I was silent for a few minutes before I spoke again. "Love-making isn't the same as true love."

"How do you know?"

"Well, for me, if I have this sort of emptiness somewhere deep inside, then I know it was just sex, and not real love. My suggestion is wait. Don't be like me, Celestia." I was trying to keep tears out of my voice now. "Be sure he's really 'the one'."

We lay there for a long while, not speaking, and then Celestia finally said, "My mom told me she wished she'd waited until she found Jon, my dad. They had to go through a lot of baggage to learn what true love was." She took a deep breath before she added, "So, how would you feel if your mother and Garek started a relationship?"

"Huh? Sorry, I was half-asleep. What did you say?"

She repeated the question.

"Oh, that. Well, it isn't as though they haven't been together at least once before."

"But it was really Martina then."

"From what Mom says, she knows she was 'there'. And why should I mind? He *is* my father, after all."

"I'm glad you feel sure now. For awhile there, you seemed hesitant about him."

"Well, like I said I haven't had a lot of good experiences with men, but I can tell Garek is a good man—the kind of man I've always thought a father should be. And I think he's good for Mom, too. She's been so alone in her life, you know."

Celestia nodded, then lay back next to me and closed her eyes. I wondered if the slight smile on her face meant she was happy this part of her 'mission' to our time was going well.

After this, I stared at the ceiling, unable to think of anything, and then trying to picture Mom and Garek together. Part of me began to ache with an intense feeling of longing. I was so tired of feeling alone in the world—like my mother—and knew what I needed was real love, too. Now, at least I had a father to love.

As I listened to the even sound of breathing, telling me Celestia and Mom were sleeping, I knew the right thing to do with my life—including James—but wasn't sure I had the strength to do it. It seemed there were urges

rising in me like a tide, even though I wanted them to
stop. So, it took me a long time to fall asleep, despite the
comfortable bed.

CHAPTER 10
THE LIBRARY

After we found a place to have breakfast the next morning, we asked the waiter if he knew of a library within walking distance. His face clouded for a moment—he apparently didn't visit libraries often—then he smiled:

"Oh, yes, there's one at the University. It's only a few blocks west of here. Just follow Bloor Street. You can't miss it. The sides are all of glass."

Sure enough, the morning sun was gleaming on the sides of a tall glass-sided pyramid, the likes of which I'd never seen. To the south of us loomed the tower we spotted our first day, but now it was revealed in its full height, pointing high into the blue, cloud-studded sky.

"That's definitely the tower we saw when we came to Tornatoh," said Mom. "And it does resemble the memories of Neptune Spire in Terres that—" She stopped there, as she saw Laken looking at her curiously. Then she added, "Uh—that Martina told me about."

As we approached the pyramid, someone was just unlocking the main door. "Good morning," she smiled. "Are you here for the library?"

"Yes, please. We'd like to look up some books, but we don't plan to check anything out," I smiled.

"That's fine, of course. You can apply for a library card, if you have identification."

We just nodded and continued inside. She would've been really surprised to see what our various ID's read. Between the six of us, we covered three different centuries.

Indoors, the sides of the pyramid rose high above our heads. A series of escalators in the middle of the vast open room went to side levels that seemed to float above us. Near the base of the first escalator was a gleaming silver-colored desk, where a woman smiled and asked, "How may I help you?"

"We're looking for a map room," Dad spoke first.

"Yes, that's the men," I nodded. "We women would like to look at a copy of the Bible, if we may."

"Of course. Gentlemen, you'll find the digital map room on the fourth level. Just go to your left at the top of Escalator Four. I'll need to escort the women to the Rare Books room."

I waved slightly to Dad as they set out for their escalator, and then turned to follow Mom and Celestia with the woman from the desk. She took us through a large set of metal doors into a glass-walled room, which had a view to the east side of the pyramid. I could tell this by the angle of the morning sun, which was bathing the room in warm light.

Then she opened a glass-walled case, and took out a large, leather-bound book with gold letters on the cover that read 'Holy Bible'. Once she'd set it carefully on a table in the center of the room, she asked:

"Do you have some form of ID I can hold while you use this room? We have to use higher security with the rare books, you see."

We glanced at each other in panic for an instant, and then I pulled out a photo card from my wallet. "I'm afraid I've let my driver's license expire," I sighed. "And the date is a misprint, but will this do?"

The woman glanced at the photo, then at me, and nodded. "Yes, that will be fine. You can get it from me when you're finished. Just come back to the main desk."

"Thank you," I said, as we all tried to smile.

Once the woman was gone, Mom asked, "What was that you gave her?"

"It really was my driver's license, but it was dated to expire in 2021. I hoped she'd accept that it was supposed to be 2121."

"That was a close one," Celestia sighed. "Let's get started before she gets suspicious."

The three of us pulled chairs close to where the book lay on the table. Mom began to gently turn through its back pages. I could tell she knew this book well and was looking for something specific.

"Here," she breathed excitedly, pointing to a section entitled *'The Thousand Years'*. "See where it says, 'And I saw an angel coming down out of heaven…He seized the dragon, that ancient serpent, who is the Devil or Satan, and bound him for a thousand years. He threw him into the Abyss, and locked and sealed it over him to keep him from deceiving the nations anymore, until the thousand years were ended'."

"What does that mean?" I asked.

"Let's read on first," she said. "It says in the next paragraph that the souls of those who'd been martyred for their faith 'came to life and reigned with the Lord a thousand years'."

"Do you think that's the same thousand years, or millennium, as the first passage talks about?" asked Celestia.

"Well, it seems logical, since they're in the same chapter, but we can't be absolutely sure. This book called *Revelation* is very hard to understand sometimes." Mom glanced up at us, as she spoke.

"I wonder," I thought aloud, "It says the Lord will reign here on earth for a millennium, and that Satan is bound in the Abyss. But what if the Abyss is the rest of space beyond the Earth? This could mean the Devil follows the people who go out from here to settle other planets in the Galaxy."

"We know for sure people will settle the Galaxy, and that as the System gains power, it will begin to deny the existence of Earth."

"That sounds like a good possibility, Ginna," Celestia nodded. "If the Devil isn't allowed to be here on Earth for that period of time, then it makes sense he would try to deny its existence. And from what my parents have said about their experiences with the System and the other planets they visited, it sure sounds like someone or something out there is trying hard to work against the King—trying to deceive people."

"I still wonder," I whispered, "Why things aren't all perfect *now* on Earth, if the True King is really in charge."

"Maybe that's what this 'millennium' is about," Mom replied. "It's giving humankind a chance to try to obey God on their own—without Satan meddling."

Celestia nodded. "Perhaps. The King's reign here could be an experiment—a sort of test of humanity's true nature. Look at this," she added pointing to the next section, titled 'Satan's Doom.' "Here it says, 'When the thousand years are over, Satan will be released from his prison and will go out to deceive the nations in the four corners of the world—Gog and Magog—and gather them for battle.' It says it will be an army beyond number, and they will attack the King."

"Where are Gog and Magog?" I asked.

"I've never heard of them," Celestia shrugged. "Maybe they could be parts of the Galactic System—wait!

Of course, that's what happened when the System quit ignoring Earth, and came back to attack it in my time."

"Which is about a thousand years from now," added Mom.

"But what should we do?"

Before anyone could answer, there came a tap on the door. Looking up, I saw the guys and motioned for them to come in, but the door was locked on their side, so I opened it.

"What was that I heard about a thousand years from now?" Laken asked, before I could even catch my breath.

"Do you know what's going to happen in the future?" added Darroch.

"We were only speculating about how a passage in the book of *Revelation* fits with what's happening now," said Mom quickly.

I nodded. "Obviously, it's a hard book to interpret if you've ever looked into it."

"I have a little," said Laken.

"So, what did you find out in the map room?" I was hoping to get off the subject of knowing the future as quickly as we could.

"We got physical coordinates for Jerusalem," Darroch smiled at me.

"What do we need those for?"

"Well, we're thinking," he continued, "Since you're so curious about the True King and his new reign—that going to Jerusalem would be a good idea."

"And you want Celestia to take us there by crossing the GAP."

"Not just that," said Laken softly, looking into Celestia's eyes. "I want you to teach me how you do it."

"I've already told you, I don't really know."

"Well, I think I may have a way to find out."

The way he was looking at her sent chills through my body. What was he talking about, and was it dangerous?

"Let's go back to the hotel and talk more about it," Mom said then, and I looked at her gratefully. "Annemarie needs to go to the front desk and get her driver's license back."

"Not that I can use it in this time," I laughed.

As we all walked out, closing the heavy door behind us, I wished I had my own copy of The Bible, feeling I was going to need to refer to it again. For the first time in a long time, I realized I needed to get back into reading it.

CHAPTER 11
INTERMEZZO WITH GINNA

Ginna sat across the restaurant table from Garek, watching his face. He'd managed to convince their younger companions they should find a club and go enjoy themselves. "Get away from us old fogies," he'd laughed. "Go dancing and have a few drinks. Quit worrying for a little while and enjoy your lives while you're young."

She could see Darroch and Laken's eyes light up at the suggestion, and her daughter, Annemarie, seemed to like the idea: "Come on, Celestia, you've been too upset about all this. Let's just have some fun for a while. It can't hurt, and it might help."

So, the four of them went a bit further up Younge Street to check out one of the night club districts. Now Garek was finishing the dinner he and Ginna ordered at a tiny café he found on a dimly-lit side street, only a short walk from their hotel.

When he set down his fork, his eyes looked up and

caught hers staring at him. "Alone at last," he whispered.

She found herself nodding. "We haven't been alone much, have we?"

Before he spoke again, he reached across the table and took her hand. "I asked you once a long time ago—though it's actually in the future—if you…"

"Could learn to love you?"

"Well?"

"Part of me wants to, Garek."

"And the other part?"

"It keeps telling me not to get hurt again. Everyone I've loved has been taken out of my life—my father, my mother, my daughter."

"But you have Annemarie back now."

"In a way, but there's been so much lost time—it's like I barely know her anymore."

"Maybe you just need to give it more time."

She nodded but didn't trust her voice to speak.

By this time, their bill was paid with a credit card Laken loaned them. He stood and helped her out of her seat. Before she could object, he'd taken her hand, and they were walking out the door. A little bell rang as the door opened and closed.

"That's a very old-fashioned touch," she said.

"Did places have those in your time?"

"A few still did."

They walked back up the side street to the main thoroughfare their hotel was on. When they came to the entrance of the Comfort Hotel, she paused and was surprised when he said, "Let's keep on walking for a bit. It's nice and warm tonight, especially for this far north."

Soon, they worked their way down toward the lakeshore. The night was clear, and stars were shining in a few places where the city's lights weren't too bright. Once they'd crossed through the tunnel and walked out into the park, they could see many more stars out over the lake.

'What should I do?' she thought. 'Why am I afraid of him? There really isn't any good reason to fear.'

By this time, they'd climbed over the tall dune barrier leading to the beach and could hear waves lapping against the shore. The moon was already high, throwing a golden beam across the water. It seemed to be pointing directly at where they stood, hand in hand. He pulled her closer and began to kiss her.

Then he drew back and gazed into her eyes. "It's a perfect night, isn't it?"

"The moon is beautiful."

"Not as beautiful as you are, Ginna."

"Oh, I'm not beautiful."

"There you go—belittling yourself again. You are the most beautiful person I've ever met in any past or future. I love you so much."

Before she could reply, he pulled her to him again, and this time he gently lowered them both to the ground, leaning her back against the dune. As he kissed her this time, she felt like she was melting into the sand.

"Long ago, in another time we did this once before," he whispered into her hair. "I know it was you all along who attracted me. Please let me have you now, with no one else in the way."

A tidal wave of warmth rose inside her, and she knew this was what she really needed. She wanted to let go and just experience this intimacy she'd never fully known before. But some doubt in the back of her mind stopped her.

"Garek, I do love you, and I know I want you. But I also know firsthand the cost of sex outside a marriage."

"What do you mean?" She was thankful to see him looking earnestly into her eyes, and not sounding angry.

"Well, I lived it almost all my life—being a single mom. And I saw the toll not having a father took on my daughter. That's probably the reason she turned her back on all I believed and tried to teach her."

Now she couldn't hide the tears in her eyes, because they were taking her voice away. He reached up gently and brushed some away. "You know I never meant to hurt you, Ginna."

She nodded. "It wasn't your fault. I was just there—by chance, in a way."

"But if we love each other now, what's so wrong?"

Shaking her head, she suddenly collapsed onto his shoulder and wept. Gently, he stroked her hair, then moved down to her shoulders, but stopped there. They lay in silence for a long time. At last, he took a deep breath and whispered, "Ginna, if I was to marry you, would that make it better?"

She sat up, looking into his blue eyes, and was surprised to see tears there, too.

"If you're really asking me."

"I'm really asking. Ginna, you're what I've been looking for all my life and never seemed to find. Will you please marry me?"

Her voice refused to respond, so she just nodded her head.

Silence settled around them. The wind became a gentle breeze, and the waves swished softly.

At last she found her voice again, "Garek, I think I've been waiting all my life for something like this, too. Is it selfish of me to want you so much?"

He laughed softly, "I don't think so." Then he drew her into another long kiss.

"You're such an awesome kisser," she said, gasping for breath. "But you make me feel so weak and breathless."

"Sorry about that," he grinned.

"So which time do we get married in? Yours or mine?"

"Or maybe this one, which is neither?"

"I have no idea," she shrugged.

"Well, it doesn't matter to me. Wherever, or whenever, you are, Ginna—that's where I want to be."

She gazed into his eyes for a long time, and he just looked back, patiently stroking her hair and smiling. At last, she moved close enough to kiss him again. "All right, Garek, I'll marry you—and I'm going to hold you to it."

"As soon as we have the chance, I promise," he smiled. "You know, I bet we can find a Justice of the Peace—or whatever they call them here—and get a marriage license."

"You'd do that for me?" Now her tears were flowing even more freely.

"Of course, I would."

"I love you, Garek, and I think you're worth waiting for, too. After all this time-jumping, what's a few more days or weeks?"

"I can't wait much longer, Ginna," he sighed, pulling her closer to him again.

Silence settled around them, and they leaned against the dune, just holding each other close. Ginna felt safe and content for the first time in a very long time. The wind became a gentle breeze, and the waves swished softly.

She whispered, "Okay, let's look for that 'Justice' first thing in the morning. But someday, I'd like to have a real wedding."

"Anything you want," he smiled.

"I'd like to have a ceremony up on one of those

mountains overlooking Salt Lake City—where it all started."

"Yeah," he chuckled. "Or where it *will* start in the future."

Again, silence settled as he pulled her to him and began to kiss her, moving down her cheeks to her neck. There was no need for any more words. Love had come for both of them, at last.

CHAPTER 12
ANNEMARIE'S NIGHT

We'd been to three different night clubs now, having at least one drink at each. I knew why Garek and Mom had urged the four of us to go out on our own.

"Just relax and try to forget all this stuff," he'd said. But I could tell he had plans of his own.

At the first place, the music was too loud, and we couldn't really talk. So, we moved up the street to the next one. Here again, the music was fast, but not quite as loud. So Laken and Darroch convinced us to try dancing with them.

I'd danced some before, but evidently Celestia never had.

"I'm sorry," she kept telling Laken each time she stepped on his toe or moved in the wrong direction. "I've never done this."

"What? They don't dance in the future?"

"I just haven't been in many cities, so no chance to learn," she shrugged.

At the end of the song, they went back to our table, but Darroch and I stayed on the dance floor for the next number.

As we danced, he whispered in my ear, "I find it interesting that Laken—who is enamored with all things old-fashioned—should get the girl from the future."

I looked up to see his eyes searching mine. "And you think you want the girl from the past?"

"The one who is sophisticated and aloof," he smiled.

"Oh, I think you're misreading me," I tried to laugh.

"And this shyness of yours is just an act, after all?"

All I could do was shake my head as he pulled me closer and twirled me to the music. When the song was over, we rejoined the others. Soon the band announced they were taking a break.

"Let's head for another place," said Darroch, draining his drink.

So, we came to this third club, one with blue lights at the windows and on all the tables. It was much quieter, too, with soft music playing from hidden speakers.

"At least we won't have to worry about when the band takes a break here," laughed Celestia. I could tell by her voice she'd been drinking a bit too much.

My head was also feeling fuzzy from the drinks, and there was something about the atmosphere in this club making it worse. "What's that funny smell?" I asked, after we'd sat for a few minutes.

"Apparently, they're experimenting with air drugs here," said Laken. "It's a new thing in the cities. There are—or were—places in Tacoma using them, too."

"None in Salt Lake, yet," Darroch sighed. "They're still pretty conservative there."

"Always have been," Laken chuckled. "Can't believe how long you've put up with it. You should've moved to Tacoma long ago."

"And perhaps died in the earthquake?"

"Oh, yeah—forgot."

Their voices were beginning to sound a little fuzzy now, too. Looking across the table, I could see Laken putting his arm across Celestia's shoulders and beginning to nuzzle her neck. Before I fully realized it, Darroch was doing the same with me.

We were all seated in a couch-like area, back in a dark corner of the club, and no one was paying attention to anyone else in the place, anyway. Before long, all I could feel was Darroch's kisses, and his hands exploring various parts of my body through my clothing. I was oblivious to whatever the others might be doing, until I heard Laken speak:

"We need to find somewhere to get naked."

"Let's head for our hotel room," came Darroch's voice. "I have a feeling Garek has his own agenda tonight."

"Yeah," came a laugh from Laken. "Let's follow the example of the old folks."

By this time, we were back out on the street, though I could barely remember leaving the club. Fortunately, the fresh air outside was helping to clear my mind a little. Then we were at the old steps of the Comfort Hotel.

I remember leaning heavily on Darroch as we made our way to their room, but the next thing I knew we were lying on one of the beds. Vaguely, I sensed Laken and Celestia in the other bed. They seemed to be whispering softly, but I couldn't understand any words.

"Come to me, sweet thing." Darroch gently pulled me on top of him. "Have you ever done this before?"

"Of course."

"I just wondered," he grinned.

As he began to slip his hands inside my tunic, I felt something I'd never felt in this kind of situation—fear—and another feeling I had no words for. Of course, I'd made love before—too many times, I realized now—but this time I kept seeing David's face in my mind. He was trying to smile at me, but his eyes looked so very sad.

Suddenly I sat up and pushed Darroch away.

"What's wrong, sweet thing?" he murmured.

"I can't do this."

"Why not? You just said you had sex before." There was a frightening gruffness coming into his voice.

"I don't know. It's just not the right thing—or the right time."

He made no reply, but I sensed the heat of his rising anger. Suddenly, he shoved me back onto the bed. Then he stood, tucked his shirt back into his pants, and stalked out the door.

I sat there shivering and pulled the blanket tightly around me, then curled up on the half-empty bed and drenched the pillow with my tears. There was no other sound but the long, low breathing of sleepers in the next bed. Perhaps something was trying to change inside me—and I hoped it was for the better. But why did it hurt so much?

***

The next thing I knew, it was morning. Laken was still asleep, and there was no sign of Darroch. Celestia was looking at me from the other bed. "Get dressed," she whispered. "Let's take a walk and get some coffee."

I smiled gratefully. Somehow, she knew I needed to talk.

Once we were out of the room and walking down the hall, I asked, "Did Mom and Garek come in at all last night?"

"No. I wonder where they are."

We didn't talk anymore until we'd reached the lobby and sat down on one of the couches, each holding a cup of coffee poured from the pot at the front desk.

"So, are you all right, Celestia?"

She nodded and stared down into her mug. "Nothing happened—I was too afraid."

"Really?" I felt myself sigh with relief.

"I feel like such a coward, Annemarie. You seem to be able to handle anything."

Tears were filling my eyes by now. "I'm so sorry, Celestia, you're really the strong one—I always seem to give in, even when I know I shouldn't. But last night, for some reason I don't understand, I didn't."

She reached across and took my hands in hers. "Don't give up. You're growing stronger, Annemarie. God still loves you."

"How can he love someone like me, who keeps running the wrong way all the time? Before this, I used the excuse that it was Mom's fault—she'd messed around, got pregnant—and so here I was, a fatherless child. I was angry and lonely, so I took it out on Mom, thinking I was punishing her by doing everything opposite of what I knew she wanted.

"But now that I know the whole story—how Mom didn't really even know how I came to be—I really feel guilty. I've been blaming her for something that wasn't even her fault. Now I don't know what to think."

We sat and sipped our coffee in silence for awhile.

Then Celestia said, "Perhaps this was a big mistake—bringing us all here to Toronto."

"Well, you didn't have much choice, did you? With looters shooting around us, and aftershocks from the earthquake."

"Sometimes that seems like it was in another life. What a mess I've gotten us into."

"You have to quit blaming yourself, Celestia. Something will work out."

"Do you think we should go to Jerusalem—like Laken wants to?"

"I don't see why not. If the King is really reigning now, there should be nothing to fear," I sighed. "But, if He *is* in charge, why do we still need police, and why are bad things happening? Should people be just having sex whenever they feel like it?"

Celestia shook her head and sipped some more coffee. "I don't know. Maybe it takes time to get the whole world shaped up. But you'd think Kristos—the one I was taught to believe in—could make it all right in an instant."

"I used to think I knew all the right answers," I sighed, "But I'm not sure of anything anymore."

Soon after this, Laken and Darroch joined us. Not surprisingly, Darroch was making a point of ignoring me. Just after the guys came from the lift, Mom and my dad walked in from the outside door, holding hands. The bright smiles on their faces told me something momentous had happened, and I wanted to be happy for them—but a tinge of envy rose in my mind. Why did I never seem to find the happiness I kept searching for?

"Okay, Mom, I can tell you've been up to something. What is it?"

She turned and smiled shyly at Garek before she spoke. "We just got married."

"How?" I jumped up and pulled her into a big hug.

"We went to the Justice of Toronto," said Dad. "Now we have a civil marriage license."

"But this is a different country," I began.

"Not anymore." Laken stepped up to shake Dad's hand. "The world is under one unity government now, remember?"

"Oh, yeah. I'm getting confused with all the Time Well stuff," I sighed.

Mom was still holding me close to her. "Please be happy for me," she whispered in my ear.

"Of course I'm happy for you, Mom. Why wouldn't I be? Maybe I'm just a bit jealous—that's all." Then I turned and smiled at my dad, and he pulled me into his warm embrace.

"You're officially my daughter now," he murmured to me.

"I'm so glad, Dad," I said into his ear.

Celestia was smiling at both of them, and even though she didn't say it, I could tell she was glad this part of her task was finally accomplished. Just as I started to say this, Darroch grabbed my waist and pulled me toward him, grinning. "Next time," he whispered. I pulled back in embarrassment, not wanting the others to see this. Pushing

Darroch away, I moved back toward Dad, and he put his strong arms around me again.

"Thanks, Dad," I sighed, leaning hard into his embrace. "I love you."

"I love you, too, Annie," he smiled.

After the others grabbed some coffee, we went to get breakfast at the same café we'd been to before. I sat as far away from Darroch as possible. Laken seemed very excited about something, but he didn't say anything until after we got our food, and begun to eat:

"I've gotten hold of the Mind Exploration Institute here in Toronto. My colleague, Tarin, still works here. She used to be in the Tacoma branch and has agreed to help us."

"Help with what?" I suspected this had something to do with his comment yesterday about Celestia teaching him to cross the GAP.

"Unlike yours truly, who is a humble police officer," said Darroch, with a chuckle, "My friend Laken is a high-level researcher in the international Mind Exploration Institute."

"So, is that how you've heard of the GAP?" asked Celestia.

Laken nodded. "It's one of the many mental phenomena we've been researching. Unfortunately, my lab in Tacoma is probably in bad shape—or I'd take you there."

"Oh, because of the earthquake," I nodded.

"Will you help me with my work, Celestia? You're just what I've been hoping for."

"I don't know. I've never been near a laboratory of any kind. I wasn't even born in a hospital."

"What kind of future do you live in?" Laken asked, in disbelief. "Sounds more like the distant past."

"Well, not everything or every place is modern in the future, just like there are remote places still here on Earth." I was hoping this explanation would satisfy them, as I cut in with this comment.

Laken nodded and smiled. "Okay, I'll accept that." Then he turned and looked at Celestia expectantly.

"I have an aversion to the word 'Institute'," she sighed. "Both my grandmothers were isolated and even tortured, in a place on Terres called 'The Institute for Rehabilitation'—one of them died there."

"But that's not the same place, sweet thing." Darroch moved toward me, and I tried to step away. Why did he call me this in front of the others? I shot a sharp look at him, hoping he got the message, and saw him smile slyly.

"I'm sure it's not the same kind of place this far in the past." As I spoke, I turned away from him and took Celestia's hand. "Maybe this will help us find our way back home."

She nodded hesitantly.

CHAPTER 13
CELESTIA AT THE INSTITUTE

Now I need to tell my part of the story, because as the strongest GAP-crosser in our group, I was the one Laken targeted. He wasn't the only one with plans, though. I guess I'd better just tell it:

After we'd all eaten breakfast, Laken and Darroch took us—Garek, Ginna, Annemarie, and me—on a tram running up Bloor Street, past the University to a blocky concrete and stone building. There was no name printed anywhere on the outside of it, and no numbers, either.

I felt a foreboding as we entered but pushed it aside. 'This is our best hope right now for finding our way back to our own time,' I told myself.

The outer door opened into a small entry area with plain white walls. There was no reception desk, just a door Laken opened by showing his eyes to an ocular scanner. I'd never seen one of these, but my parents had mentioned them before.

With a series of clicks, the door's locking mechanism opened. Laken smiled and took my arm as we all walked into a long white hallway, brightly lit by overhead lights. After walking past at least a dozen doors, we turned toward a gray-colored door on our left. Again, he used an ocular scanner to access this room. Inside was a circle of blue-gray chairs and a very long table covered in white material.

Standing beside the table was a small pale woman with short purple hair. As soon as she saw Laken, she nodded and smiled, "It's good to see you again, Laken."

"Tarin, thank you so much for coming to help us," he said, quickly embracing her. "This is Celestia. She's also studied the GAP."

Tarin's eyes were quite curious as she turned and looked at me. She seemed to want to ask me questions, but took a deep breath instead and silently shook my hand. Her fingers felt cold—even icy.

"Pleased to meet you," I murmured.

An awkward silence filled the room, so I turned and introduced my companions, just to break the stillness.

"Where are you all from?" she asked. I wondered if she realized what a loaded question this was.

"I met them in Salt Lake," Darroch spoke up. "Then we all went to Tacoma to meet Laken."

"Unfortunately, an earthquake arrived shortly after they did," said Laken. "And I brought them here—to safety—with Celestia's help."

Tarin turned back to stare at me, but I just nodded, thankful Laken hadn't mentioned the GAP-crossing to her.

My eyes were beginning to tire from all the unaccustomed lights and whiteness, but then Tarin turned and tapped a switch on the wall which dimmed the lights. My knees began to quiver in fear, and I sank into one of the chairs. "Will this hurt?" I heard my voice ask. "Why must we do this, Laken?"

"I'm sorry." He took my hand. "I thought you wanted to help me."

I glared at him. "I'm not even sure I like you. I tried to tell you last night."

He backed away in surprise, but Tarin stepped up and took my hand. "You're just stressed, Celestia. Please trust me—everything will be fine." This time her hand didn't feel so cold, but as she was saying this, I felt a needle-prick in my arm.

"What are you doing?" I heard Ginna demand.

"I'm just giving her something to help her relax," came Laken's voice, which seemed to be moving farther and farther into the distance.

The next thing I knew, he was maneuvering me onto the long table and connecting a single cord to my forehead. "We used to have to connect all kinds of electrodes to do this, but now we only need this one." Then I couldn't hear any more voices at all. They were drowned out by a humming in my head.

This sound wasn't really in my ears but somewhere inside my mind. It changed pitches periodically, from a low rumble to a higher ringing sound. I could see lights above me on the room's ceiling but found it more comfortable to close my eyes.

Then I began seeing things through Laken's eyes. Pictures from his mind jumped into my brain—his reaction to my refusal to make love the night before—scenes of our flight from his flat in Tacoma—and the memories of things he'd experienced before we met. Images came of people who must have been his friends—occasionally I saw Darroch's and Tarin's faces among them. I saw him working in a laboratory similar to this one, and dimly sensed other minds he must have bonded with before.

Vaguely, I wondered if this was anything like what my mother and Ginna experienced when Jon brought their minds together in one body. But I still felt my own body. I could sense Laken's head just touching the top of mine, and my back felt the unyielding hard white table.

'Perhaps this isn't quite the same,' I thought. 'They continued to move and live, and—yes, even make love. I feel more like I'm in a state of suspended animation, knowing where I am but not able to take any independent action.'

Then I felt something sharp and cold probing into my mind. I wanted to pull back and cry out for it to stop, but my body gave no response to my mind's attempts to move.

The feeling was like a steel knife moving ever so slowly into the depths of my thoughts. My mind was screaming, but no sound came from my mouth. Then just as suddenly as it started, the pain stopped. I found myself lying on the table, looking up at the ceiling, and gasping for breath.

"Celestia—" Ginna's voice seemed miles away. "Are you okay?"

I tried to nod, but my body still wouldn't respond to my mind.

"What have you done to her?" another voice demanded, but I couldn't tell for sure who it was.

"She'll be back with us soon." This I recognized as Laken's smooth voice. Now it had an oily sound that turned my stomach.

I have no idea how much time passed, but then someone was holding my right hand. At last, I could feel my own chest rising and falling, and knew my mind had finally regained control of my body. I blinked my eyes, slowly turning my head toward the right. Ginna's face was looking at me with deep concern.

"Are you all right?" she whispered.

I nodded slowly and tried to get my lips to move. It took several tries before my voice could find its way back out of my chest. "I'm back."

"We were so worried," came Annemarie's voice. "If anything happened to you, it would've been my fault for convincing you to do this."

"She'll be fine now," said Laken. I closed my eyes so I wouldn't have to see him. I'd been inside his mind, and I couldn't face him yet.

"He saw my mind, and I saw his," I whispered. "Was that what it was like for you and my mother, Ginna?"

"Maybe a little. But it wasn't painful, and I could tell you were in pain."

"Yes—cold steel—pain." I wanted to turn and stare at Laken as I said this, but I found it hard to look at him. "Did you get what you wanted?" I asked.

Laken nodded, but it was Darroch's voice I heard, "Yes, we did."

I turned my head to glare at him, and he dropped his gaze to the floor. Then, looking more closely at Laken, I saw his face did look pale. Perhaps the experience had also been painful for him. Part of me hoped this was true—he deserved it.

"May I please be alone now?" I asked.

Ginna stood and nodded. "If that's what you want."

"Someone should stay with her," said Laken softly.

"I'll stay, Mom," said Annemarie. "You and Dad should take a walk and get some fresh air. You both look tired."

"Laken and I need to talk," came Darroch's voice.

Soon Annemarie took the chair on my right, gently holding my hand. "Just try to think of your favorite place, Celestia. Imagine yourself in the one place in the Universe you'd most like to be."

I closed my eyes and tried.

CHAPTER 14
SUPER-SONIC TRANSPORT

A new day was dawning as warm sunlight poured into a shadowed room. Where was I? At the Institute? In the hotel? Home in the cave, with my parents? I really had no idea and lay for awhile in total confusion.

Then I felt Annemarie shift and move in the bed and realized we must be back at the hotel.

"How did I get here?"

"You don't remember?" Ginna asked.

"Not a bit. I remember Laken took me to that place, and there was pain—so much pain I want to forget."

"They say it will pass," she sighed. "I hope they're telling the truth."

"Did Laken learn what he wanted to know?"

"He says he now understands how you cross the GAP."

"Are they still talking about going to Jerusalem?"

"Yes."

"So, will we cross the GAP to get there?" asked Annemarie.

"I don't think I have the strength to do it right now," I sighed.

"For some reason, Laken decided to get us all tickets on an air-transport," Ginna replied.

"So maybe he realized he still doesn't know enough to do a GAP-crossing himself." It made me feel good somehow, that he hadn't been able to extract enough information from my mind. And I vowed I wasn't going to give him another chance, either.

"We have one more day for you to recuperate, Celestia," Ginna added. "I think we should take one of Laken's credit cards and go shopping for some new clothes."

"Shopping? I've hardly ever done that."

"Oh, it'll be fun," said Annemarie. "Besides, we need clothes that will be better in Jerusalem's climate. It's very different from here in Toronto."

***

The shopping was fun, as we walked up and down the busy city streets, ducking into this shop or that. It was another warm summery day, and the breeze off the lake was just right to keep us feeling comfortable in long-sleeve cotton tunics.

"It'll be much hotter in Jerusalem," said Annemarie. "We need to get some long, light-weight dresses to cover up with, to protect ourselves from too much sun but still keep cool.

Most of the shops in Toronto didn't seem to have this kind of clothing, which was understandable. Finally, though, we found a little shop with signs in Arabic above the English and French ones. Here we tried on several types of things the attendant called 'kaftans'. I chose one with stripes of maroon and pink running through the white and cream muslin. Ginna liked the brown one better, and Annemarie got one with yellow and green stripes. Each had a fabric belt to tie it up, more like the tunics I was accustomed to. But without the belt, it flowed freely down from my shoulders to my feet, with a swishy comfortable feeling—nice and airy.

Early in the afternoon, we met the men at the hotel, and Laken announced our flight arrangements were made.

"We'll be taking one of my company's SST's," he smiled.

"You're kidding, right?" Darroch exclaimed.

"No, really. The twelve-passenger one had six seats open, so I got permission to use them, said we were all doing MEI research."

"M-E-I?"

"That's Mind Exploration Institute—remember, Celestia?" whispered Ginna into my ear.

"Oh, yeah, how could I forget?"

"Don't worry," said Laken, apparently hearing our exchange. "Your memory will return fully in a short time."

"It'd better," Ginna retorted, glaring at him.

"Anyway," he resumed, "Our trip to Jerusalem is part of the research because while we travel, I'll be studying my notes on what I learned yesterday." He glanced at me, and I felt an involuntary shudder. "Hopefully I'll be able to bring us back by crossing a GAP."

I said nothing in response to him and just looked at the floor.

"What's an SST?" asked Annemarie, to change the subject.

"You've never heard of a Super-sonic Transport?" Darroch's voice was incredulous.

"Actually, I have," said Ginna. "They were tried in the second half of the Twentieth Century, but were grounded because fuel costs were too high to make them worth it."

"Well, now we have much better sources of fuel than petroleum," Laken smiled. "Almost all air-transports are SST's now. They fly in the stratosphere, so there's less air resistance. Going faster than sound, we'll get to Jerusalem in about five hours. Have any of you ever flown in one?"

"I did a couple of times," said Garek, "When I worked with the Forestry Commission."

"So, they still have forests in the future, huh?"

"Yes, Darroch, they manage to conserve a few, especially since they stopped using trees to make paper."

"What? Aren't there any books in the future?"

"It's all on computer terminals," I said. "Except a few antiques. My father had one antique book that was very precious to him." I stopped suddenly, wondering why I was referring to Dad in the past tense, when he was actually far ahead of us in time. "I mean—he will have it—in the future."

I saw Garek turn and smile at me, and then I felt too confused to remember the rest of what I was going to say.

"Well, let's get all your gear packed," said Laken. "We're due at the air terminal in two hours, and with this city traffic, we need to get started as soon as we can."

"Packing won't take us long," I laughed. "We originally set out on this journey with only about two-days'-worth of supplies."

The three of us decided to go ahead and put on our new clothes.

It was easier to roll up the hiking clothes and stuff them into our packsacks, since it didn't matter if they were wrinkled. The kaftans felt like they'd be more comfortable for travel in a transport, since we'd be seated most of the time.

***

The air-transport terminal was a frenetic place. Large and small vehicles buzzed around on the ground and hovered in the air, both inside and outside the building. Huge windows let in the scene from outside, so the inside of the terminal seemed twice as busy.

We were taken there in a hover-taxi, which was sleek and brown, with plush beige seats for each of us. Once inside the terminal, Laken guided us into a quiet waiting area with black leather couches—much like the ones we'd seen at his flat in Tacoma. It hit me then:

'Since we left there so suddenly after the earthquake, he has no idea what shape his flat is in now. Maybe I'm being too hard on him. He may have lost everything, but he seems to be trying to help us. Of course, he has his own agenda, with this MEI research. Still, I'm not sure I'd be able to concentrate on work, knowing my home was probably destroyed. Perhaps working is his way of coping—either that, or he's obsessive about learning to cross the GAP.'

As we lounged in the private waiting area, he and Darroch were talking quietly to each other and looking closely at a tablet screen he held. Ginna and Garek sat close together on one of the couches, while Annemarie and I lay back in some really comfy lounge chairs and closed our eyes. My head still ached some, an echo of the intense pain I felt during the mind-reading process. I tried to do some deep breathing and relaxation exercises my Aunt Daiah, had taught me—or rather, that she would teach me in the future. What a paradox!

After about half an hour, we heard a chiming sound and a voice announced, "Our MEI transport is ready for boarding, sir."

Laken quickly turned off his tablet and jumped up. "Okay, folks. We're going through this center door."

Following closely behind him, we passed through a security check. Even though no one was visible, some kind of force-field surrounded us as we went beyond the door. After walking down a short hall, we found ourselves moving through an oval door, turning right into a long tubular-shaped room with pairs of seats on each side of an aisle.

"I've never been inside an air-transport before," I whispered to Annemarie. "Is this what one looks like?"

She nodded. "The ones in my time are longer and more crowded, though. This one is a really upscale version of the planes I've seen."

"We don't even call them planes, anymore," added Darroch.

A smiling flight attendant directed us to take the seats closest to the rear of the tube. Laken and Darroch took the back seats to our left. Ginna and Garek seated themselves directly across from them. That left Annemarie and me to take the set of chairs in front of Laken and Darroch. This meant we couldn't see the faces of any of our companions, but I soon realized we might be able to hear some of what the two behind us talked about. 'This might come in handy later,' I thought.

Soon there came a humming sound as the SST's engines revved up, and it began to move into position for take-off.

"This is a lot quicker than flying commercially," Garek said. "We're getting the VIP treatment."

"I've never flown before," added Ginna.

Just then, the engines began a loud roaring sound, and I felt myself being pressed back into the cushions of my seat. Faster and faster the SST went, and suddenly we were airborne. It was a strange sensation to see the ground rapidly falling away from us out the windows. I pressed my face to the thick glass of the small oval window, trying to recognize any landmarks below. Lake Ontario seemed to disappear in an instant, and then we were moving up through fluffy gray and white clouds. After that, all I could see was the clouds' upper surfaces, looking like puffs of cotton or wool, with the deep blue-black of the stratosphere above us.

With nothing else to look at, I soon lost interest and lay back in my reclining seat, closing my eyes. I must have fallen asleep because the next time I looked out, patches of blue water appeared through occasional breaks in the clouds.

"That must be an ocean," said Annemarie, looking out over my shoulder. "We've been flying over it for nearly an hour."

"Wow! How long did I sleep?"

"Around two hours. But you didn't miss anything." She gestured toward the seat behind us as she said this. "They've been sleeping, too."

'Well,' I thought, 'Perhaps his experiment took a lot out of Laken, as well.' Somehow this made me feel better.

"Which ocean do you think this is?" I asked.

"Well, I'd say Atlantic, if we've taken a southerly route. But I can't be sure. In my time, planes taking off from Toronto would often fly over the North Pole and the Arctic Ocean to reach Europe. It was actually a shorter route. Back then, you could tell the Arctic Ocean by all the ice. But who knows in this century, with much of the polar ice cap gone?"

"So, I guess we just enjoy the view," I smiled.

She nodded, and we kept watching to see if anything besides the blue waters would appear far below.

I began to doze off again, when she suddenly pointed, "Look, land!"

There was indeed a patch of grayish-green on the horizon, and it seemed to be getting bigger even as we watched. We were traveling so fast and high, however, it almost flashed by. Then we saw what looked like a blue sea or large lake, followed by a wide expanse of yellow-brown.

"I'd be willing to bet that's the Sahara Desert," we heard Garek say behind us. "It's grown a lot since your time, Ginna. Now it covers Africa almost all the way down to the Equator."

"That means the lake we just saw was the Mediterranean Sea," said Annemarie.

"We'll be over Egypt soon," I heard Darroch say.

"We're going too fast to see much, though," Laken added.

Apparently, they'd just recently awakened, too. So, we wouldn't hear much conversation from them, after all. Maybe they'd purposely avoided talking—to prevent us from eavesdropping.

Now, we continued our gradual descent, as the desert below us became a bit more distinct. Still, it was mostly an empty expanse of sand, dotted here and there with some rocky hills and outcrops. As soon as I saw a line that might be a river, we banked to the northeast and followed the edge of the body of water called the Mediterranean.

The engine sounds changed as we dropped ever closer to the ground, and then I saw what looked like a city—a vast area of gridded roads and tiny blocks of buildings. An open, wider road appeared in front of us, and I realized it must be a landing strip.

A new sound startled me, but Annemarie just smiled. "That's the landing gear deploying."

There was only a slight bump as we touched down and slowed to coasting, moving along the ground toward a low building with many large windows.

"Welcome to the Holy Land," said Laken's voice behind us. "The cradle of the world's great religions, and now the capital of the world, at last—ruled by the True King."

I could hardly believe my ears.

***

Once we got off the plane, we were shepherded

through another posh waiting area. No one here seemed to be concerned with checking for ID's—and I heaved a sigh of relief, since I didn't have anything at all to show.

'This must be Laken's doing,' I thought, 'Or his company's.'

As we left the terminal building, there were monorails humming overhead, and hover-craft darting all around the entrances. Laken took us directly to a waiting white hover-craft with room for all six of us. It appeared he knew the driver, so I assumed this was also part of his Institute's arrangements.

We glided low over walled fields looking like vineyards, based on pictures I'd seen in Dad's copy of The Book. Darroch pointed to a terraced hillside:

"That area has been growing olives for centuries."

There were low dwellings and tall high-rise buildings between the fields. Then suddenly, it seemed the structures took over the land, with nothing but buildings as far as my eyes could see.

"Welcome to the City of Jerusalem," said Laken.

The hover-craft slowed because there were so many other vehicles rolling and buzzing around us. It seemed a miracle there were no collisions.

I think I held my breath all the way through the next few minutes, until we finally settled to the ground in front of a tall marble-fronted building. "Is this a hotel?" I heard Ginna ask.

"Yes," smiled Laken. "The original King David Hotel,

now restored after the Unification Wars. From here you'll be able to catch glimpses of the New Temple."

I saw Ginna and Annemarie look at each other in surprised disbelief. "So it really does happen—they *do* rebuild the Temple," whispered Ginna.

"Come on, let's go to our rooms," said Laken, ignoring her comment.

Suddenly I felt my blood run cold. What were the rooming arrangements going to be here? After what happened in Toronto, I had a bad feeling I knew.

As I expected, Laken walked right up to the front desk and said we had three rooms reserved.

"Yes, sir," the clerk nodded. "Each room has two single beds."

"What?" said Darroch in surprise, looking at Laken curiously.

"That's what your company always reserves, sir," the clerk looked confused. "Is there some mistake?"

"Oh, no—everything is fine," smiled Laken.

I saw Garek glance sidelong at Ginna, but she just shrugged and smiled, "We are married now." Then they signed for the first room. But I was even more surprised when Laken and Darroch signed for the next room together.

"Here, Celestia," he handed the stylus for the computer-pad to me. "I thought you and Annemarie would like to have some space to yourself."

"Thank you, Laken," I whispered.

"It's mid-afternoon here, so you have time to freshen up and relax a bit first. One of us will contact you when we've made dinner reservations," he added.

The glassed-in lifts were very fast, and before we knew it, Annemarie and I were each lying on our own cushy-soft bed.

"I could get used to this kind of travel," she sighed.

"I'm still wondering what their hidden agenda is, though. They didn't go to all this trouble—with the company SST, and all—just for a sight-seeing jaunt."

"Yeah. And I keep wondering how a 'humble police officer', as Darroch calls himself, gets to do all this traveling with a person like Laken."

"Darroch does seem to have another personality when Laken is around. Do you think maybe he's like a bodyguard?"

"Well, that's a possibility. They seem to act more like close friends, than co-workers. But there's something creepy about him," she muttered.

I closed my eyes, feeling the pain in my head coming back. "Well, all we can do is wait and see, I guess. Right now, I'm going to try some more relaxation breathing."

CHAPTER 15
THE OLD CITY

A knock on our door woke both of us from a deep sleep.

"Hey!" came Ginna's voice. "Don't you girls want some dinner?"

Blinking, I tried to remember where I was—and when. 'Oh, yes, Jerusalem, in the Twenty-second Century—2123.'

Annemarie opened the door, and the rest of the party entered our little room. She dashed into the bathroom, and I was left trying to make my hair look like something other than a bush. I rummaged through my packsack for quite some time before I found my hairbrush.

"You look fine, Celestia," said Laken's voice. He moved close behind me and squeezed me around the waist. "I like long, dark hair." He grinned and pulled his long ponytail onto his shoulder to show me he'd braided it.

"Well, just let me use the bathroom and I'll be ready."

I stepped out of his hug and quickly ducked in as soon as Annemarie came out.

Soon we were down in the heat and bustle of the city. We didn't have to walk very far before we saw several restaurants, each specializing in a different cuisine—from Turkish to Russian, Greek to German.

"This city really is the capital of the world," Garek laughed.

"I've read that it's been like this for centuries," Ginna replied. "A city has stood on this site for over four thousand years. I love to read ancient history."

"This city will still be here in the Thirty-first Century, if I remember correctly," said Garek. "But it won't be the world capital then…"

I heard him stop in mid-sentence and saw him glance at Laken and Darroch. I was hoping he hadn't revealed too much about the future again.

"Then it will be five thousand years," I murmured. "It seems almost impossible to fathom."

"Does this mean some of these streets and buildings are that old?" Annemarie asked. She had let her long blond hair down, since she'd had more time to get ready in front of a mirror than I did. In my mind, I told myself not to envy her good looks.

Meanwhile, Laken turned to her and said, "Jerusalem has been attacked, destroyed and rebuilt several times—Jebusites, Israelites, Babylonians, Romans, Crusaders, Turks—and probably more through the ages."

We were walking east and could see the rays of the setting sun behind us, reflecting off the columns being built to support the new Temple.

"Two or three Jewish temples have been built on this same site, I think. It's called Mount Moriah," Laken continued.

"Each temple was eventually destroyed, wasn't it?" I said.

"Historians record that Herod's Temple, the last one, was destroyed by the Romans in 70 AD, on the same day of the same month—in the Jewish calendar—as Solomon's Temple was destroyed by the Babylonians in 587 BC. Isn't that eerie?" Ginna added.

"Sure is," said Garek. He was holding her hand, like he almost always did since their marriage in Toronto.

"And there was a mosque on the site for over a thousand years, too," added Laken.

"Will we get closer to see the new Temple?" I asked.

"Perhaps," he smiled at me.

By this time, we reached a German restaurant, where the guys had made our reservations. Soon we were seated and ordering.

"I haven't heard of any of these," I sighed, as I tried to read the menu. "Does anyone have a suggestion?"

"My favorite is wiener schnitzel." Darroch pointed to the words on the page. I noticed that though it was spelled with a 'w', it was pronounced with a 'v'-sound.

Once the food was ordered, I could tell Ginna was anxious to ask a question, "One thing puzzles me, Laken. Why are police still needed, and natural disasters—like the earthquake—still happening? If the True King is now reigning over the whole world shouldn't all that be over and done with?"

"Well, it takes time for a new political leader—whether he's king, president, or premiere—to get everyone to obey."

"But if he's really God, can't he just make it all happen at once?"

"Well Celestia, I suppose he could," Darroch put in. "But for some reason, he wants us to obey of our own free will—not just by force."

"But he may resort to force with some of the more violent offenders," added Laken.

"Why?" I was getting confused.

"Well, in this time, he's come as the political Messiah the Jews have been looking for—not just as the Savior who died for the world's sins, like he did the first time."

"I don't see why the Temple needs to be rebuilt," Ginna spoke up. "The perfect sacrifice has already been made, when God's own Son offered himself up for all time. So why go back to the old way if the new has already come?"

None of them seemed to know how to reply, and a heavy silence descended for a few minutes.

"And what about the other religions?" Garek finally broke the silence.

"They're waiting for the final judgment, when their good deeds will be weighed against their bad ones. Their fate, they believe, is determined by that tip of the scales," said Darroch.

"And I take it this final judgment hasn't come?" I said, glancing at Ginna and Garek. I wondered if they were remembering the conversation we had about even our good deeds being like filthy rags in God's eyes.

Soon our food arrived, and we began to dig in. Laken kept staring at me with his dark, slanted eyes as we ate, and I wondered why.

As soon as our main courses were finished, the waiter brought a cart of luscious desserts, and we couldn't resist ordering something. I got one called Black Forest Cake, with lots of cherries.

"I have one more question," Ginna said, between bites of her apple strudel. "When did construction start on the new Temple? And what happened to the mosque?"

"Well, the True King appeared in 2112, just eleven years ago, and declared the new Kingdom of God here on Earth, with its capital here in Jerusalem. One of the first things he did was start building the Temple. The mosque had already been destroyed by Tarshiesh."

"And the Muslims didn't revolt?" Annemarie asked.

"Of course they did, but that was all back during the Wars of Unification." Darroch smiled. "Now the new

King has restored the sacred stone, where the prophet Mohammed traveled to heaven, and enshrined it inside what will become the inner court of the Temple."

Ginna was shaking her head. "But I thought it was the Anti-Christ who was going to build the Temple, and then later desecrate it."

"That's how some people have read the prophecies," said Laken, "But time has shown this interpretation to be incorrect."

"Laken, I believe they're thinking of when the Romans desecrated and destroyed Herod's Temple in 70 AD," added Darroch. "But scholars now believe the prophecies in the book of *Daniel* were pointing to the Maccabean period over 500 years before the Romans. The Temples on this site were desecrated several times."

"I sure wish I knew more of this history," I sighed. "The System has kept so much hidden from us."

"The System?" said Laken and Darroch together. "What's that?"

"They're in the distant future," Garek said. "After humans have settled many other planets."

I found myself wishing I had a copy of The Book—to see if what they were saying was really true. Something still didn't seem right about all this.

Laken was giving me a strange look. Suddenly, he got to his feet. "I'll take care of the bill. How about if we walk off some of this rich food and head toward the Jaffa Gate?"

"Where's that?" I asked.

"Just a little way up this road. It's one of the gates in the walls of the Old City."

Soon we were trudging up and down the hilly streets, toward the imposing stone walls. Then a tall gate with intricate stone-work and towers came into view.

"Was this wall here in Christ's time—or King David's?" asked Annemarie, awe in her voice.

"No, this one dates from more recently. It's part of the Roman Emperor Hadrian's reconstruction of the city, in 135 AD."

Laken nodded. "Right, Darroch. Like most ancient cities, it was attacked, torn down, and then rebuilt right on top of the previous city's rubble many times."

By this time, we'd walked through the gate, and once inside the city walls, we could see a street stretching straight out in front of us.

"This is definitely Roman," said Darroch. "See how straight it is? "Most of the lanes and side streets of the Old City wander and wind at random."

Laken added, "This is called King David Street."

The signs we saw were mostly in Arabic or Hebrew, rarely in English. After we'd walked a short distance on King David, he turned us off into one of the narrow winding lanes. There were stalls with people selling almost anything imaginable, from raw meat to trinkets. Most of them appeared to be the lower front floors of the owners' houses.

I was beginning to feel overwhelmed by all the noise and smells, and grabbed Laken's arm to keep from fainting. He wasn't my first choice, but was closest to me. He just smiled and put his arm around my waist, and I didn't mind too much, since he was keeping me on my feet.

"This city is like a window on the past." Ginna's voice sounded excited. "It seems like we've walked into ancient times."

Laken was nodding. "Over the centuries, the rulers change, things are torn down and built back up, but humans just go on scratching out a living."

"I wonder if things will change with the new King," I mused.

"Time will tell, I suppose," he said to me softly, pulling me closer.

After we'd wandered the narrow lanes, and up and down some side streets which were really staircases, we finally came to an open, flat paved area. On the far side of it was a very old-looking wall, made of massive stones.

"Is this the Wailing Wall?" Ginna said, awestruck.

"Sure is," smiled Laken.

We could see men dressed in black robes standing with their heads against the wall, apparently praying. Above them were scaffolds around what would be the New Temple someday.

"I'm still confused," said Ginna. "Why do they need to keep wailing at the old wall, when the Temple is being built?"

"I think they're praying for the New Temple," said Darroch.

"Do Believers come here, too?" I asked. Somewhere in my mind, I was hearing a verse that said something about Believers being built into a true temple.

"Now they do. The Old City used to be divided into four quarters, but now those barriers are gone. All have been brought together under the True King." Darroch was smiling as he said this, and had a faraway look in his eyes. But whenever he moved toward Annemarie, I saw she was doing her best to avoid him.

Ginna's face was still puzzled. Moving away from Laken, I went to stand closer to her. "What's wrong?"

"It just doesn't fit with what I was taught," she shrugged. "But maybe back in the late twentieth and early twenty-first centuries, there were some things people didn't know yet, and so they misinterpreted the scriptures."

"My dad once told me prophecy was like looking at a mountain range from a distance," I said. "When we're far away, all the peaks look about the same distance from us. But as we travel closer, some that seemed close turn out to be much further on than we expected."

"Sort of a trick of perspective?"

"That's a good way to describe it, Ginna." Then I whispered to her, "Still, I agree—something's not quite right here."

The shadows were lengthening, and the men moved back closer to us.

"We should probably head back to the hotel," said Darroch. "All the shops are closing, and soon the streets will be getting empty."

I wondered to myself if there were still dangers in the dark—even here in the Holy City, supposedly ruled by the True King. Now I knew even more clearly why Ginna was feeling confused.

***

The next morning, we all met in the lobby and had breakfast in a small café right there in the hotel. The meal turned out to be some flatbread and a grain called couscous, very unlike all the eggs we'd eaten when we were in North America.

As soon as we finished, Laken paid the bill and announced he wanted to take us to the MEI offices here in Jerusalem. Suddenly, I felt my insides begin to quiver. What was he up to now?

The Mind Institute offices were in the newer northwestern part of the city, so we were able to take a monorail to get there, a nice change from walking.

I noticed many broken places in the streets' pavements, as we rode along high above them. As we skirted around some sections of the northern Old City wall, I could see spots where it had been recently torn down or even blasted apart. But there were few signs of anything being repaired.

"What happened there?" asked Annemarie, before I could speak.

"Those are left from when Tarshiesh was fighting to hold the city. But of course, there was no stopping the armies of God," smiled Darroch.

"It must have been quite a fight, to do all that damage," said Garek.

"Well, we *have* evolved beyond battering rams and siege engines, you know," Laken laughed.

"I'm still mystified as to why there was so much fighting. Why couldn't God just appear and put a stop to all of it?"

"Who are we to question God, Celestia?" I heard a sharpness in Darroch's voice I hadn't expected. "He does what he does for his own reasons."

"Yes, we know," I said quickly. I was trying to think of some way to change the subject, but Ginna did it for me:

"I'm wondering if the eastern gate—the one they called the Golden Gate—has been opened yet. It was sealed shut with solid stone walls in my time and had been for centuries."

"Of course," said Darroch, looking at her in surprise. "That's the gate the King entered through, just as it was foretold."

Now Ginna was smiling. "Now this does agree with what I was taught. How did they do it, Darroch?"

"Well, Tarshiesh was actually the one who blasted it open, when he destroyed the Dome of the Rock. And when the King came, he walked through the original Golden Gate site, just as he'd ridden through it on a donkey the first time he came to Earth."

"I know that story well," said Annemarie. "We call it Palm Sunday."

I was still wondering if all this was somehow a trick—was this King really the True Lord? But looking at their excited faces, I could tell this wasn't the time to bring it up. Just then, Annemarie caught my eye and nodded to show she was feeling the same way.

By this time, we'd reached a very new section of the city, where high-rise buildings pierced the sky, their bright metallic sheens threatening to blind me. At last the monorail stopped, and we all stepped off. There before us was a façade of golden-colored glass with the emblem of MEI emblazoned above the door. Looking up, I saw the building was topped by a large purple sphere. I'd never seen anything like it. Compared to the unmarked MEI building in Toronto, this was obviously meant to impress.

I tried not to shudder as Laken led us through a slowly revolving door that never stopped turning. He just nodded and smiled to the person at the reception desk and took us toward the lifts.

Stepping inside the first open set of doors, he pushed a button marked with a cryptic sign instead of using any of the usual floor numbers. It seemed a long time before the lift moved. I grabbed hold of Annemarie's hand as the sliding doors closed. "Don't leave me alone with them," I whispered hoarsely.

"Don't worry, Celestia, I won't. We'll all stick together this time."

Ginna turned slightly toward us and nodded her agreement but said nothing. I realized she'd been staying close to Garek all morning, often taking his hand.

Our ride in the lift was long enough that I knew we were headed for the highest floor. Sure enough, when we stepped out, we were surrounded by lavender light, and the curved walls of the vast open room were shining purple as the sun hit them. The scene through those windows was breath-taking, and my three companions were drawn to look out.

To the east, we could see the raised platform where Solomon's original temple had been—and where there would be a new one again soon. Beyond this was the city wall, with its newly reopened Golden Gate. The Kidron Valley disappeared into shadow behind the wall, but the Mount of Olives rose up beyond it, catching the midday sun. When I turned and looked to the southeast, there lay a vast desolation of hills and valleys stretching as far as I could see, until they disappeared in heat haze.

"That's the wilderness," said Laken, who stepped up close beside me.

"Where Kristos' cousin John preached and baptized in the Jordan River," I nodded.

"And where Satan temped him while he was wandering there for forty days," Ginna added.

Garek was standing next to Ginna, following our gazes. "I wish I'd learned some of this when I was young," he sighed. "There weren't very many Believers left by the time I was born."

Laken and Darroch looked at them with puzzled looks. "What in the world are you talking about?" asked Laken.

I cringed. Somehow, I knew they shouldn't learn too much about the future.

"Never mind," I laughed, trying not to sound nervous. "Can we get a tour, Laken? This place is the most amazing thing I've ever seen."

He grinned broadly and took my hand. "Sure, let's get started, Celestia."

We walked through several rooms clustered around the edges of the sphere. There were no ceilings in them, so they opened to the purple dome above us. Some of them looked like offices, with desks and terminals, while a couple had those ominous long white tables that I remembered too well from Toronto.

The last stop we made was in front of a door marked in bright red letters, "Classified. Restricted Area. No Admittance".

"Sorry we can't go into this one," Laken said. "But I hope to get my clearance soon."

As we walked away from the door, back towards the lift, I saw Darroch glance back and wondered what he was looking at. When he saw me watching, he shrugged, smiled, and moved to put his arm around me. 'Why is he doing this?' I wondered. 'Is he trying to make Annemarie jealous?'

Then, as he tightened his grip on me, I felt a strange lump under his left arm. Just then, the lift chimed and the doors slid open. He quickly dropped his arm, and we all stepped inside. Holding my breath, I tried to calm myself. Not only was Darroch creepy, but now I was sure he was carrying a weapon.

The rest of the day, we took a monorail tour of the city with a guide who told us about various landmarks. It was amazing to think the Lord himself had walked in this place millennia ago. I knew the stones of the oldest streets and buildings had been torn down and built up many times since then, but there was still some kind of awe about being in Jerusalem.

We were hot and tired by dinner time and decided to just grab a bite at the café in the hotel—where we'd started our day with breakfast. No one mentioned any evening plans, and I wasn't at all anxious to spend the evening with Laken or Darroch, so I said to Annemarie:

"I'm much too tired for any night-life tonight. How about you?"

"Same here, Celestia. I think I'm just going to turn in early."

Laken was looking at us almost sympathetically, though Darroch was definitely miffed.

We all stood as soon as the bill was paid, again by Laken, and set off toward our respective rooms.

"Whew," Annemarie said, once we were safely inside our door. "Things about Darroch are beginning to scare me."

"Me, too. For one thing, I'm pretty sure he's carrying a pistol in a shoulder holster."

"Really?"

"I could feel it through his jacket when he put his arm around me, there by the lift."

"Well, we did wonder if he's Laken's bodyguard. He *is* a police officer, after all."

I was shaking my head though. "There's still something off about him."

Annemarie looked down and sighed. "Mostly, he acts like a typical self-absorbed male as far as I can see, and I want nothing to do with him. I saw how he tried to move in on you to make me jealous."

"Well, you have no competition from me," I laughed. "And I guess the bodyguard idea helps me feel a little better. But I have a big fear of guns, you know. Only the System Patrols have them in our time. So, whenever I see someone with a weapon, I automatically think 'enemy'. I know you have other reasons to fear Darroch, and I'm sorry I let us get high that night in Toronto."

"It's my fault as much as yours, Celestia. But I know one thing for sure—I'm definitely not going to sleep with him," she sighed. "What about Laken? What do you think of him?"

"Laken is a real mystery to me," I went on. "Sometimes I fear him, too. I don't want to go through that mind exploration ever again. But other times, I get this feeling he really wants to help us. I just don't know what to think."

"Well, at least he was gentleman enough to let us have this room to ourselves," she smiled.

"Yes, that *was* Laken's idea, wasn't it?"

"I don't know about you, but I'm going to take a nice hot shower and then crawl into this comfy bed."

"Go ahead," I smiled. "My turn is right after yours."

CHAPTER 16
LAKEN'S SURPRISE

The next morning, we did our usual breakfast. I keep forgetting to mention how odd I found it sitting on a chair at a table nearly waist-height. In my time, tables were low and close to the floor, so people could sit cross-legged, or even recline on cushions while eating. I was gradually getting used to sitting up at a table, but my back was often sore.

Once we were finished, Laken took us to the monorail. It was a cloudy day this time, so the city didn't shine like the day before. "Looks like we may get a little rain later," said Darroch, settling himself beside me on the cushioned seat. I tried very hard not to move away from him, but he made me nervous.

"Are we going back to MEI today?" I said casually.

Laken, who was seated directly across from me, nodded. "Celestia, I need to know more about how you travel in time."

"No!" I said and would have jumped out of my seat, if Darroch hadn't put his arm across my lap and held me down. "You can't force me—I'm not your slave," I added between gritted teeth.

Darroch almost looked like he wanted to handcuff me. Then Ginna's voice came from the seat in front of him:

"I think I can help you more than Celestia, Laken." I wondered at how calm she was managing to keep her voice. "I've traveled a great deal in many GAPs, both in time and space."

"That's impossible," scoffed Darroch. "You're from the past."

"No, actually, it's not." I could tell she was going to reveal our secret, but she was looking at me intently now, and I knew she was determined to do this.

"Mom, are you sure you should tell them? What if it changes the course of history?"

"Well, so be it, Annemarie. Perhaps this is how the true powers of the GAP are discovered—who knows?"

By now Laken's eyes were wide with wonder. "Please tell me what all of this is about."

While the monorail moved almost soundlessly through the city toward the purple-topped MEI building, Ginna told the whole story:

"When my brother and I were young teens in Colorado, back in the early Twenty-first Century, we were visited by two time-travelers, Jon, who is Celestia's father, and Jael, her uncle. They came and took us into their story. I can't really explain how it worked, but we seemed to experience their lives with them.

"The second time they came, just a few years later, Martina was with them, too—that's Celestia's mother. This time Jon explained we lived in parallel universes, and he took my brother and me into the bodies of Jael and Martina. We 'became' them—in their world and time—and experienced *everything* they did. Sometimes we could even communicate with them in our thoughts.

"We moved back and forth between our worlds a couple of times, and actually lived nearly four years of their time. But each time Jon brought us back, it was the same night we'd left."

"I can't believe this."

"Sh, Darroch," Laken hissed. "Let her finish. I've read some articles on String Theory where physicists have proposed this very thing."

"Well, the best proof I can give you that all this really happened is sitting right here—my daughter. You see, I was a virgin when Jon took me 'into' Martina. And when he brought me back, I was pregnant. About nine months later, Annemarie was born, and I became an unwed mother."

"But how does that prove anything?" It was hard to tell if Darroch really didn't understand, or if there was something else he was angry about.

"I had no idea who her father was, because in my own body, I never had sex with anyone." She glanced shyly at Garek.

"I can vouch for that," he said softly.

"Twenty-five years went by, but then Celestia showed up at my front door, not too long ago. She suspected that when her mother, Martina, had an affair with Garek, while I was ''inside' her, somehow I got pregnant."

"You're telling me that a man from the Thirty-first Century got you pregnant, and didn't even know it? That's about the craziest story I've ever heard," Darroch scoffed.

"We thought so, too," said Annemarie evenly. "But after we went to Celestia's time and found Dad-"

"Which wasn't easy, by the way," added Garek. "They all put themselves in great danger to do it."

Laken was staring in awe at Ginna and Garek. Then he looked at Annemarie, and nodded to himself, seeming to recognize the family resemblance. "You're certain this is what really happened?"

"Absolutely certain," Garek said. "I can't really explain, but even though I'd never actually seen her, I somehow recognized Ginna when I met her. And by the way, it hasn't been a case of her throwing herself at me, either—quite the opposite, in fact. But I think we've finally worked things out." He took her hand and smiled.

Ginna nodded but seemed at a loss for words now.

"Wow!" said Laken at last. "So, can I learn from you, Ginna, how this joining of you and Martina worked?"

"Perhaps," she nodded. "I don't really understand it, and I can't explain it."

"Just like I couldn't explain how I cross the GAP," I added.

"But perhaps you can find at least some of it in my mind."

I reached across the aisle and took her hand. "Ginna, you don't need to put yourself in danger for me—not like this."

But she shook her head. "I'm still hoping perhaps Laken will learn something to help us get back to our proper time."

I knew by the look of determination in her light brown eyes that there was no changing her mind now. Perhaps she was hoping to find some answers for herself, too.

By this time, the monorail was slowing for the station adjacent to the MEI building. Laken rose excitedly and led us all back inside. We again took the lift to the spherical room at the building's top, but this time, two people in white lab coats met us as we exited. Soon they put us in one of those side rooms with a long white table. My blood ran cold and I shivered involuntarily.

But now it was Ginna who lay on her back, head-to-head with Laken. I was feeling queasy just watching, and finally had to excuse myself. Annemarie came out the door close behind me, looking very concerned.

"She *will* be all right, won't she?"

I nodded. "I came through, didn't I? All I got was some headaches."

She sighed, and I hoped she realized I was trying to tell her the truth.

"You mother is a strong, determined woman, and I think she really wants to see if she can find a few answers of her own through this."

"I just wish we could go home." Tears were beginning to shine in the corners of her eyes.

There were no words I could say to help. I just hugged her and joined in with a few tears of my own. 'It's all my doing that we're here,' I thought. 'I'm the one who brought them to my century, a time of danger and tribulation for Believers. And the one who tried to take them to the Fountain, and got us sucked into this Time Well, instead.'

Finally, we seated ourselves on one of the low couches, along the walls made by the side rooms. We could still look up and see the sky through the purple-domed roof. Water drops were beginning to spatter the glass of the orb. Whoever said it looked like rain today was right.

***

We'd been sitting for what seemed a long time when Garek came up to us, looking very distressed. "Annemarie, come quickly. Ginna's in a coma, and Laken thinks only a blood relative can bring her out of it."

I jumped up too fast and felt dizziness threaten to drop me to the floor. Annemarie had already let Garek take her hand, and they were running toward the lab's door. I managed to squeeze in just behind them before the door clicked shut—and probably locked.

Laken was no longer connected to Ginna, but he looked very pale himself.

"What went wrong?" I asked Darroch, thankful for once that he came close, as soon as he saw me.

"Laken thinks it was too much information for Ginna to relay to him. He was getting overloaded and had to terminate the connection. We think that's what sent Ginna into a comatose state."

I found myself getting so angry I wanted to pound Laken with my fists, but instead I turned away from him, staring at Ginna's pale form on the dreaded white table. Remembering the pain I'd felt, I wondered if this was part of the problem, too.

"Is there something you can give her for pain, Laken?"

"Why?"

"Because your mind-exchange process hurts like hell!" I shouted into his face.

"No one has ever told me that."

"Did you ever think to ask?" I snapped. "I don't know how many other people you've done this to, but it sure hurt me. I had headaches for days afterward."

"I'm sorry, Celestia. I wish you'd told me." Then he

stood shakily and turned to a wall cabinet which he opened with a key. Taking out a small vial and a syringe, he filled it and injected something into Ginna's arm. "There, that should help."

"What is it?" I demanded.

"Good old-fashioned morphine. Seems nothing works better, even with all our so-called progress."

Just then I felt the room begin to spin around me and my knees gave way. Darroch caught me just as I started to fall, and set me on a bench along one of the curved outer walls of the room. He sat down next to me and began rubbing my arms and legs, then my back and neck. "Try to think calm thoughts," he whispered. "You're just having an anxiety attack."

"Well, I think I have good reason to be anxious right now."

Meanwhile, I hadn't seen what Annemarie and Laken were doing. It appeared they'd put together a mind connection between daughter and mother.

"I tried to connect with her, but it didn't work," Garek was saying. "Please, God, if you're real, don't let me lose her now—after finally being with her again."

His plea faded into silence, and none of us could think of anything to say. We watched anxiously, as Annemarie began to speak softly:

"Mom, it's me—your little girl. Remember? We didn't always have it easy, but we always had our love for each other. I know how much you gave up for me—by letting me be born. There's no way I can ever thank you enough. Please don't leave me now. I was wrong to shut you out of my life for so many years. But, Mom, it was myself I was angry with, not you. Please…come back."

Her voice faded to a whisper, and then all I could see was her lips moving in thoughts.

The silence seemed to hang like dark webs in the corners of the room, and in our minds. But there was nothing I could do except pray. I found it a hopeful sign, as I thought about it, that Garek felt the same urge.

Then suddenly, Ginna let out a loud gasping breath, which was echoed by her daughter.

"A—Annie?"

"Yes, Mom, I'm right here with you—I promise to never leave you alone again."

"Oh, so many mistakes I made. I'm sorry, Annie."

"Was I a mistake, Mom?" Annemarie's voice was tight and full of emotion.

"No, never! Somehow I always knew you were meant to be—my only child."

Ginna's eyes opened then and I knew she was staring at the ceiling like I had on the white table in Toronto. But this room was open to the dome, and had no ceiling. I found myself glancing at the purple dome above us. Then I followed her gaze as it shifted to Garek.

As soon as he saw her eyes begin to focus on him, he

jumped to her side and grabbed her hand. "I promise to never leave you, either." He knelt beside her, stroking her hair. "Please promise you'll stay with me."

"I promise."

It wasn't until then that I heard a deep sigh of relief from Laken. He stepped over to the table and held up another syringe.

"What's that?" demanded Garek.

"It's a small dose of adrenalin—to get her bodily functions jump-started."

"Are you sure you know what you're doing?" I could see Garek had his doubts, with good reason.

"Yes, I know. I've done this many times before in my research. It's just Ginna and I had an information overload because there were two people's memories stored in her mind, instead of just her own."

"So, you experienced Martina's memories, too?"

"Yes, Garek, and I know what happened between you." Laken gave a slight smile. "The good news is—now I *do* believe your story about how you got Ginna pregnant, even though you'd never met her."

Darroch rose from the bench and helped me to my feet. "She's going to be all right now. I think we should leave Garek and Annemarie with her. Laken, are you coming?"

"Just as soon as I check her vitals. I can't afford any more mistakes."

Shortly after we'd walked back into the large central part of the dome, Laken joined us. We all sat down wearily in some large chairs arranged in a semicircle.

Darroch spoke up first. "Did you get what you were looking for, Laken?"

"Yes, I understand how the GAP works, and with help from another first-born, I think I can do it." He smiled at me as he said this.

At first, I looked away, still angry. But then I turned back and looked him in the eye, as I asked, "So now do you think you can help us get back to our own time?"

"I think it's a good possibility. But there's one more thing we must do first."

"What's that?" asked Darroch.

"Go to the Moon."

"The Moon? You mean Earth's moon?"

"Yes, Celestia. I'm sure you've seen it," he smiled.

"Of course I have. I was born here on Earth, even if it *is* a few centuries from now. But why do we need to go to the Moon?"

"That's where MEI's most advanced and most secret laboratory is located."

"You've never even told me that."

"And I probably shouldn't be now either, Darroch."

"So, how do we get there?"

Laken didn't answer him but turned back to me. "Have you ever been in space, Celestia?"

I shook my head. "My mother and father have, but not me."

"Yes, I have many of Martina's memories of their travels, but she's not first-born. I was hoping for some help from you."

At this, I jumped out of my seat and began to pace. "Now, wait just a minute!" I shouted. "You've put me through torture—and now nearly killed my mother's friend. What makes you think you'll get me near any more laboratory tables again? Why should I help you?"

"Because I'm trying to find a way to get you four back home."

"Okay, Laken." I sat down in another chair, a bit closer to him and farther from Darroch, because I didn't like the way he was looking at me. There was a glint in those dark eyes, but I couldn't tell if it meant I was turning him on—or making him angry.

'This is strange,' I thought to myself. 'Here I'm beginning to feel I trust Laken more than Darroch. I didn't trust either of them before, and Darroch is supposed to be a police officer.'

"In the very top of this dome, there's a small silver sphere," Laken's voice came into my thoughts. "Look up, now that the sun is low. Can you see it?"

I glanced up and did see *something* up there.

"It's a prototype spaceship—similar to the one your parents used to flee from Terres."

"You got that far back in Mom's memories?"

He nodded. "And I've recently been given all the basic training and security clearance that goes along with piloting this ship. The only missing piece was knowing how to cross the GAP—and now I have that—thanks to you and Ginna."

"When do we start?" I said grudgingly. "Perhaps if we can find a way back home, it will be worth it."

"As soon as Ginna is feeling better, we'll set the plan in motion. Right Darroch, my friend?"

"Absolutely," nodded Darroch. But he still had a strange look in his eyes.

CHAPTER 17
A LONG-LOST MEMORY

After her ordeal at the Jerusalem MEI Institute, Ginna decided to room with her daughter and me for a couple of nights.

"It's not that I want to be away from you," she told Garek. "But I don't know what strange things my mind might blurt out, and I just feel more comfortable with my daughter."

His eyes clouded a little at her first words, but then he smiled. "Okay. I think I understand, Ginna. Just remember I'm always here for you, if you want me."

He pulled her into a tight hug, which she returned, leaning her head on his shoulder. "I'll be back to normal soon, I hope," she murmured.

Luckily, we had two large beds in our room, so she and Annemarie were able to share one, and I still had the other one to myself.

Sure enough, somewhere in the dark of the first night

with us, she sat bolt-upright in bed and began crying, "No, Tim! I don't believe you. This is impossible!"

Rubbing my eyes, I turned to Annemarie in confusion. "Who's Tim? What is she talking about?"

"I think Tim was my Grandpa Parker's name. I never met him."

Ginna's voice began again, this time a bit more calmly. "Why are you doing this to us? Danny and Ginna need a father. And you're bailing out in the most selfish way I've ever heard of."

"Mom?" whispered Annemarie. "Are you here? Who are you talking to?"

Ginna turned and stared at her daughter blankly. "What? Was I talking in my sleep?"

"I guess so, Mom. You said something to Tim. Who is he?"

"Tim was my husband."

"But Mom, you weren't married until we found Garek. Maybe you were talking to my grandfather?"

Ginna put her head in her hands, rubbing them through her short, brown hair. "Yes, I remember now. I'm *your* mother, aren't I?"

Annemarie nodded. "And now you're married to the man who is supposedly my father—Garek Carson."

"That's right. I remember now. I must have been in a memory of my own mother's. Your Grandma Lauren."

"I guess the mind-sharing with Laken has reawakened

old memories," I said, moving closer to them by sitting on the edge of their bed.

"It's all sort of blurry," Ginna sighed. "I have a feeling this memory is one I buried very deep in my subconscious."

"Was it a painful one?" I asked.

"Must have been," said Annemarie. "You were sobbing so hard."

Ginna sat in silence for a few minutes, trying to stop crying. "I think I remember what it was now. I can see it all in my mind, as though it's happening right here, this moment." She closed her eyes, then opened them as she began to speak:

During my pregnancy (with you, Annemarie) was when Mom dropped a bombshell on me. One day, as we were fixing supper and Danny was away at soccer practice, she turned to me with a determined look on her face.

"Ginna, there's something I have to tell you. I just can't keep on bearing this alone."

By the stricken look in her eyes, I thought I was in big trouble. What had I done wrong now? So I was taken completely by surprise when she said:

"You know your father left me for a lover, right?"

I nodded, feeling confused. This wasn't news to me.

"What you don't know, Ginna, is that lover was another man."

I almost dropped the bowl I was mixing biscuit dough in. "What?"

"A man, Ginna. Tim told me he realized he was gay—that he had been all along."

"But you two were married. You had Danny and me. How could he change like that?"

"I have no idea. It took me completely by surprise. I never saw it coming."

By this time, tears were streaming down her face, and I set the bowl down to give her a hug.

"I still don't know if it makes me feel better, or worse," she sobbed.

"You mean because it wasn't another woman?"

She nodded silently. I pulled a napkin off the table and handed it to her to dab her tears.

"I've heard people say it's just how they were from birth, Mom. Maybe some people have a different set of hormones, or something."

"But does that really make it normal?" she sighed. "I mean, some people have brain chemical imbalances that make them obsessive or paranoid. Does that mean they're 'normal', too?"

"Gosh, I don't know, Mom."

"She looked at the floor and said nothing for a long time.

I moved my arms to her trembling shoulders. "I can see how much you're hurting, Mom. I wish there was something I could do."

"Of course, it hurts," she said at last. "It's turned my whole world upside down. I've had to re-examine everything I thought I believed."

"How did you keep this to yourself all these years? I mean, the divorce was over five years ago."

She hung her head and shook it. "I didn't want you to go through all the extra confusion and pain. The divorce was hurtful enough."

"But you shouldn't have to bear things like this all alone, Mom."

"I guess that's why I had to tell you. With what you've been through now, I hoped you'd understand at least a little."

I pulled her into a tight hug. "I love you, Mom. And now I guess I understand why Dad has cut himself off from us."

"I'm so sorry he did that, Ginna. I wish he hadn't, but I guess he just couldn't handle it."

I just sighed. Now it was my turn to wipe angrily at tears. "So, what does all this mean?"

"I don't know, Ginna. Nothing we do or say can change anything."

"If God is so good, why did he let this happen?"

She stared at the floor for awhile before she answered. "There's no way for us to know—mere humans that we are."

"It's so unfair!" I realized I was staring down at my pregnant belly as I said this. "And don't say, 'Life isn't fair.' I'm sick of hearing that, Mom."

"I know," she sighed. "So am I. Not long ago, I read a book that said, the Lord doesn't promise us an easy life, but he does promise to walk with us through whatever comes."

"You've read a lot of books like that, haven't you Mom?"

She merely nodded.

"I have a lot in my bedroom, if you're interested." She almost managed a smile. "And please don't say anything about this to Danny. I'm not sure how he'd take it."

"You're wondering if he might be like Dad?"

"It's crossed my mind, I must admit."

"Don't worry, Mom. This will be just between us."

Gratitude glowed in her eyes.

Annemarie and I sat in silence after Ginna finished reliving all this.

"Well, now I can see why your mind covered over this memory, Mom."

Ginna again sat with her head in her hands, tears dripping between her fingers. "I wish I'd never remembered any of it," she sobbed.

Annemarie and I were on either side of her, but at a loss for words.

"Maybe now, though, I can let go of it forever," she sighed. "I pray it never comes back to haunt me again."

"That's right, Ginna." I patted her shoulder. "This past is long gone."

"I hope so. The divorce and my unexplained pregnancy were all I could handle back then. It took all my strength just to make it through one day at a time. My mother and I grew much closer after this, though. And that did a lot to help me. That's the only memory I want to keep—my mother's love, and how she managed to pick up the pieces of a shattered life and go on."

"I wish I remembered Grandma Lauren more," sighed Annemarie. "I was only nine or ten when she died, wasn't I?"

Ginna took her daughter's hand. "That was another of the unfair things of my life. But I still had you." Her voice broke then, and I wondered if she was thinking about how Annemarie had been shutting her out recently.

"I'm so sorry for turning my back on you, Mom. I wish I'd known more about this. Maybe I wouldn't have been so selfish."

They sat holding one another's hands for several minutes. "Well, you're back now, Annie. And that's all that matters anymore."

CHAPTER 18
ON TO LUNA

I was afraid it would take a week or more for Ginna to heal from her ordeal, but she said she felt much better after only a couple more days.

"Are you sure you're okay?" I kept asking.

She jumped up and laughed, "I said I feel fine, didn't I?" The look in her eyes said somehow she'd come to terms in her own mind over the situation with her father. I wondered to myself if she'd buried it again—or perhaps by telling it to us, she'd been able to just let it go and actually forget.

"Now, can we please get on with this big plan Laken has?" she broke into my thoughts.

"Mom, we haven't told you anything about it. How do you know?"

"Well, I don't know the details, I'll admit, but anyone with any sense at all can tell something's up. Where does he want to take us next?"

So, what else could we do but congratulate her on her perception? And tell her the details we knew.

The next morning, Laken took us all back to the MEI building for the last time. Now he had the code to open the door labeled 'Restricted Area.' Here, he helped us all get outfitted with the spacesuits we'd need for the flight to the Moon, or Luna Station, as he called it. We all were sworn to secrecy—that if we ever did get back to Earth in this century, we weren't to tell anyone of the existence of this MEI facility on the Moon.

Once we were suited up and briefed on what to expect, Laken flew us in a small hover craft which moved inside the dome. Very expertly, he brought it to a stop at the loading port beside the airlock of the silver sphere. Seeing it up close like this, I could tell it bore some resemblance to the Terresian ship my parents had told me about.

As we stepped through the outer door of the airlock, I noticed there was room for three of us at a time to acclimate. Our suits began to provide what our bodies would need in the non-pressurized interior of the ship. Once my group—Laken, Darroch, and I—moved from the airlock into the center of the ship, the other three could enter.

"This part is different from the Terresian ship," I said, knowing that now my voice was carried by the com-units in our suits, since there was no air to carry the vibrations. "My parents' ship had a pressurized hold."

"Well, as I said, this is a prototype," Laken replied. "Some of those details will come later."

Soon all six of us were seated in our appropriate launch chairs. Most of these were a pale blue color that I knew would be associated with the Star Corps in the distant future. Laken, however, took the chair with gold-colored upholstery, and indicated he wanted me in the seat next to him, which was green.

He laid his arms full length along the arms of his chair and settled his palms over some sensors at their front. From Dad, I knew this was how he became 'imprinted' into the ship's navigation systems.

"Prepare for take-off," he smiled at me.

"What am I supposed to do?" I was totally clueless about how any of this worked.

"Just follow my directions, if I ask for help."

"Uh—Okay."

Above us we heard a strange sound, but Laken told us it was just the top of the purple sphere opening.

"Now, be sure your safety harness is all buckled," he said. "Then lean back into the cushion of your seat. They're specially designed to help absorb most of the G-force. Here we go." Then he closed his eyes.

It felt like something very heavy suddenly sat on my chest, but as I leaned back and took long slow breaths, I felt better.

In another instant, I opened my eyes and saw the

most amazing sight. Earth was far behind us now, looking like a small blue marble. In front of us loomed the barren silver-gray surface of the Moon. Scenes of craters, mountains, and vast empty plains slid past us.

"We're on impulse power now," said Laken. "Soon, we'll be going around to what people used to call the dark side of the Moon—the side which always faces away from Earth."

"It isn't always dark, though, is it?"

"That's right, Ginna," he nodded. "When the Moon is full—from Earth's point of view—then, yes, the back side is dark. But during other phases of the moon, it's partially and sometimes fully lit."

"But everything is the opposite," added Annemarie. "Now I get it. Our new moon is the dark side's full moon."

By this time, we were moving into darkness, and it was harder to see what was below us. "We chose to come on a full moon—from Earth's point of view—so we're less likely to be seen by prying eyes," said Laken.

'This place must be really Top Secret,' I thought, just as a strange shape began to loom out of the shadowed mountains.

"There it is, folks. MEI's secret outpost."

Then he closed his eyes again, and before I knew it, our ship was resting in a nest-like cradle made to keep it level to the ground.

"Whew!"

"Are you all right, Laken?" I noticed he looked pale.

"The first time I ever did that."

"Well, I'm glad you did it, since you were using us as guinea pigs," said Darroch, sounding angry.

"Guinea pigs?" I asked. "What do pigs have to do with it?"

"It's just a saying, Celestia," Darroch laughed. "It means we were like his laboratory test subjects."

I saw Ginna and Annemarie nodding. They must have heard this phrase in their century.

Meanwhile, Laken unbuckled his harness, so we did the same. This time, there was no need to wait in the ship's airlock because we were still going to be using our suits when we stepped onto the Moon's surface.

And when we did, I felt a strange thrill. This place was like nothing I'd ever seen before, covered with a fine, floury dust. Since there was no air or wind, our footprints would remain there forever—until someone else stepped on them or rubbed them out.

"This is the ultimate desert," I heard Annemarie's voice say in my com.

"That's for sure," said Ginna.

"There's no water at all here," came Garek's voice.

"No atmosphere either," added Darroch, "So no precipitation of any kind ever falls."

"And no atmosphere means no wind to blow the dust around either."

We tried to look at each other as we talked, but the faceplates on our helmets were coated with reflective material to protect our eyes from the unfiltered rays of the sun. Since this side of the Moon was in darkness, we were using artificial light from headlamps on our helmets.

Laken motioned for us to follow him toward a low ridge. Walking was a very strange sensation in the one-sixth gravity of the moon, more like leaping or taking very long giant steps. Soon we saw the manmade shape we'd seen from space. It was a long low building, mostly masked from view by the ridge behind it.

Once we passed through the airlock of this structure, we were relieved to get out of the suits and helmets. The building was very similar to the ones we'd seen in Toronto and Jerusalem. The long white hallways with doors on either side made me fearful, but I tried not to let it overcome me.

Laken seemed to know exactly where he was going, so we followed. After passing several doors, he stopped at the first one with a nameplate on it. I couldn't read the name, though, because it was in some foreign script.

As we stepped through the door, a tall woman with burgundy-red hair stood up behind her desk.

"Laken, what are you doing here?"

"Good day to you, too, Mauren," he chuckled. "I thought I'd let you know that I just crossed the GAP to get here."

"You what?"

"You heard me—I crossed the GAP."

"But how?"

"Just the way we've always calculated it would work, my dear. This young lady is Celestia." He pointed to me. "She has the ability, and was kind enough to let me search her mind."

"Oh, is that so?"

I nodded and looked down at the floor.

"Where are you from, Celestia?"

I wasn't sure exactly what to say, but Laken summed it up in one of his calmest voices, "She's from about nine hundred years in the future, Mauren."

"He's kidding, right?" Mauren looked directly at me, and I had no choice but to answer:

"No, Ma'am. It's the truth. My three friends and I got sucked into a Time Well."

"What's a Time Well?"

"It's one of the dangers of time travel we haven't even encountered yet, Mauren."

She sank back into her chair again, shock on her face. With a vague wave of her hand she indicated we should sit, too. There were a few soft chairs near her desk, and the men helped the women get settled. Laken remained standing, though.

"So, what illegal thing do you propose to do *next*, Laken?" Now Mauren's voice seemed to suddenly turn cold.

"I know it wasn't in the current plan. But the opportunity dropped right into my lap—or rather right into my flat in Tacoma—when Darroch brought these four to see me, after they told him about their crossing the GAP."

"And you thought you'd just push ahead on your own?" Now she was talking through clenched teeth.

"I *thought* you'd find my discovery fascinating."

There was a tense silence, and then she cracked a small smile. "I must admit I do find it almost unbelievable." She glanced quickly at Darroch as she said this.

Then she finally took a closer look at the rest of us, where we sat opposite her desk, trying not to look as fearful as we felt.

"I think all of you should get some sustenance and rest. Then we'll talk more. Darroch, you stay."

And with that, she turned back toward her terminal screen. Apparently, we were dismissed.

As we filed out her door, leaving Darroch behind, I heard Annemarie whisper to her mother, "Whew, I feel like I was just in the principal's office after getting caught skipping school."

Ginna patted her on the back, "Me, too, Honey— though I never actually skipped school. But once I got called to the principal's office for fighting on the playground."

"You, Mom? Fighting on the playground?"

Ginna laughed. "That story will have to wait for another time."

As we walked down the hallway, I could see a very puzzled look in Laken's eyes, so I asked, "What do you suppose she wants Darroch for?"

He shook his head slowly. "I have no idea, Celestia. I didn't even know they'd met."

"She knew him by name, though," said Ginna. "That seems very strange."

"Especially for someone who says he's just 'a humble police officer'," Garek added.

"I have a bad feeling about this," Laken sighed.

None of us knew what else to say, so we followed him as he took us into a reception area.

***

We were given small sleeping quarters, a single room each. It felt very strange to be alone in my bedroom. How long had it been since I'd slept this way? Usually, there were at least three of us to a sleeping area, in the cave or the huts of my Uncle Darien's Safe-Zone. Suddenly, I was very lonesome for my family, and it settled as a deep ache in my heart.

I wasn't yearning for any special person, just companionship, but for some reason Laken came into my mind. It wasn't his body I desired, though—it was just the presence of a friend. Since Darroch was now revealed to be a 'friend' of Mauren's, there was something even more sinister about him that I couldn't put my finger on.

I must have finally fallen asleep, for when I woke all the lights were darkened. Since 'days' lasted about twenty-nine Earth-days on any given point of the Moon, they were apparently using artificial lighting to imitate the rhythms humans were used to on Earth.

Something made me rise from my bed and test the door. I wouldn't have been surprised to find it sealed from the outside. But when I gently pushed on the handle, it opened. Now curiosity took over as I tiptoed down the darkened hallway. There was still a bit of light from the red exit markers. It seemed all buildings had these, no matter the planet or the era.

As I padded gently on the white tile floor, I heard voices and froze in mid-step. They were coming from a door just ahead and to my left, one of them sounding like Laken.

"What do you think will happen to us?" I knew this was Darroch. I'd heard him in many settings by now.

"I'm disappointed in Mauren's reaction," Laken was saying. "I thought she'd be excited at this breakthrough in the project, but she seemed angry instead. By the way, how do you know her?"

"Oh, I met her a long time ago. She was just passing through Salt Lake, and we met at a bar."

The tone in his voice sounded evasive, and I wondered if Laken could hear it, too. A long silence indicated he was probably confused about Darroch's actions and wasn't sure what to say next.

"Maybe, she doesn't like the idea of us getting all the credit for the discovery," said Laken at last.

"Well, perhaps. But I've never taken her for that sort of person." There it was again, another hint Darroch knew Mauren well. "Still, people and their hidden agendas can surprise you."

Darroch's voice faded to a whisper, and I couldn't hear anymore without getting dangerously close to the door. I decided I'd better get back to my room before anyone discovered me out here.

Back on my bed I wondered if we were in danger here, after all. 'Why does this world, if it's ruled by the True King, seem so off-kilter? These times aren't any different from my Thirty-first Century life—except that Believers aren't being persecuted, at least not openly.

'Now I'm totally confused. Is everything my parents taught me just wishful thinking? Is there really a better time and place somewhere in the future? They searched the Galaxy to find a better world, but it sure doesn't seem to be here on Earth.

'What about this vision of Heaven they often talk about?' I said to myself. 'Ginna's even seen it, through my mother's eyes, and she seems totally convinced it was real. Will I ever get to experience this place? Why did I fail in my GAP-crossing?'

I closed my eyes and tried to envision myself falling asleep. Even if I didn't actually sleep, I could still try to relax and hopefully clear my mind.

Early the next morning, according to the artificial lighting, I set out from my room to see if there was any tea or coffee to be had. Sure enough, I smelled the aroma of coffee around a corner of the hall and stepped into a room looking like a small café. Laken was seated alone at a table, so I joined him.

"Morning, Celestia," he nodded.

"Good morning, I think."

"Did you sleep well?"

"No, not really."

"Perhaps you were missing a warm body beside you?" He was smiling, but it wasn't the leer I expected when I looked up at him.

"I guess I already know *your* thoughts on that," I whispered.

"And I saw yours, too," he smiled again. "You almost gave in, you know."

He looked closely at my face then, and I knew he could read what I couldn't bring myself to say. My mind went blank with him looking at me that way, so I concentrated on sipping the hot coffee. At last I mumbled, "Maybe we should just forget the whole thing ever happened."

"Okay, Celestia, if that's what you want. We'll wait and see if you change your mind about me. After all, I've seen into many of your thoughts."

For an instant, I felt my old anger begin to flare, but when I looked up, I was surprised to see a hint of regret in his eyes.

"I'm sorry I put you through all that, Celestia. I was being selfish—thinking only of my research."

"Well, I had hopes of finding a way back to my time. That's the only reason I agreed to it in the first place."

"And that was Ginna's reason for permitting my second attempt."

"So, *did* you find out anything to help us?"

"Well, I got us here by crossing the GAP."

"That's true, Laken." We sat in silence again, and then he got up from his chair.

"Would you like something to eat, Celestia?"

"Sure. Do they have any of those eggs?"

He chuckled. "Those would be difficult to get all the way out here to the Moon—too expensive. No, I'm afraid all we have is previously frozen pastries."

"I'll just have whatever you are." I started to get up from my chair to follow him, but he motioned me to stay seated.

"I'll get some for both of us." When he smiled down at me, I found myself smiling back. Maybe he wasn't such a bad person. After all, he hadn't been angry or forced himself on me, when I turned him down that night in Toronto.

Just as we finished our pastries, the others wandered in, looking quite sleepy-eyed too. Darroch seemed to be the only one who was his usual alert self.

Then, after we'd eaten, two guards entered and walked directly over to our tables. "Come with us, please," said one. I could tell by his gesture that he meant all six of us.

Feeling very uneasy, we followed them out into the hallway. As soon as we left the eating area two more guards fell in behind us. This did not look good.

Soon, it was obvious we were being escorted back to the office where we'd met Mauren. When we reached the door, one of the guards in front of us stepped aside and stood at attention. The other one led us inside, while the rear guards followed us, the last one stepping into place on the other side of the door. Then the door clicked shut ominously.

Mauren was standing very stiffly this time, and her face looked like a cold marble statue. "I've been informed by headquarters your flight here was unauthorized, Laken."

"It took them that long to find the ship was missing?" Laken seemed to be trying to make light of her accusation, but I could see his sarcasm wasn't what she wanted to hear.

"I can see you're still as self-possessed as ever." Her voice was getting louder and angrier now. "You've gone too far this time though."

"So, are we under arrest?" Laken seemed to still be trying to smooth-talk her.

"Yes—all six of you. I have corroboration of your actions in Toronto, too—from Tarin. You'll be sent back to the King's prison in Jerusalem."

Suddenly, I saw Laken's mask of self-confidence fall away, and fear was written all over his face. "But my friends are innocent. They had nothing to do with my crime."

"That's not what you bragged yesterday," she said coldly. "You mentioned mind-exchanges with one of them. Besides, they were all with you, so that makes them accessory to the crime." Now she turned to one of the guards. "Take each of them back to their sleeping quarters—and this time, lock them in. We'll prepare the shuttle for departure and be rid of them by the end of today."

I noticed a very surprised look on Darroch's face as the guards led us away. He tried to glance back at Mauren, but a guard shoved him ahead. Apparently, he wasn't expecting to be locked up, too.

CHAPTER 19
UNDER ARREST

That day seemed to last forever. I cried until I had no tears left, regretting I caused my friends to suffer this fate. As time dragged on, the only thing I could do was stare at the floor. Now I knew what total despair felt like.

As the artificial daylight was beginning to dim for Luna's 'evening' my door suddenly opened and one of the guards we saw in the morning came into my room. Quickly he pulled me to my feet and tied my hands behind my back.

"That's not necessary," I said through gritted teeth. "I have nowhere to run."

He didn't speak a word, just pushed me roughly out the door. There hadn't been much left in my pack-sack, but now it was left behind. I knew better than to ask if I could have it.

Soon we were joined by the others, each with their own personal guard and their hands bound like mine. The doors of a shuttle bay slid open as we approached them, and an ominous-looking cavern of a room was revealed.

Inside was a shuttle craft looking similar to the SST we'd flown to Jerusalem. But this one seemed larger, at least from the outside. All six of us were shoved into the airlock. Our guards didn't follow us, but they did cut our bonds.

"They mean for us to suit-up ourselves," Darroch grumbled, almost to himself. "Too lazy to help us. I can't believe Mauren betrayed me like this," he added in a whisper.

When we stepped out of the airlock into the shuttle's main cabin, I expected to see more guards, but there were only the pilot and his assistant. I glanced at Laken and saw him nodding to Darroch and Garek. Perhaps there was a chance to overpower them. But Darroch shook his head and motioned for us to take our seats. I wondered what he was up to now.

As the engines powered up, I could tell this was an old-fashioned rocket-powered ship. I'd read about these in school. No GAP-crosser was needed to pilot it, but it would take us about three days to reach Earth at its top-flight speed. The rocket power was only needed to get us out of the Moon's gravity. Then the momentum of the ship would carry us toward Earth, as long as we were aimed in the right direction. Smaller rocket thrusters could help make course corrections and position us properly for re-entry into Earth's atmosphere.

Once, we were in space, we were allowed to get out of our helmets because the cabin was pressurized, though there was no artificial gravity. Perhaps this technology wasn't developed yet.

It seemed like our spacecraft was drifting aimlessly. I'd never experienced this type of travel, having always been on the surface of the Earth, or crossing a GAP. It was an eerie feeling of vertigo, compounded by the lack of gravity. Whenever we left our seats, we floated weightlessly around the cabin.

Time ticked slowly by, but there was no way to mark it. I was used to going by the position of the sun in the sky. Now all I could use was the ship's chronometer, which apparently was set to Greenwich Mean Time. I had no idea how this time compared to where we were going.

Eating was a strange experience, too, with the lack of gravity. Our food came in clear tubes we sucked from, hopefully not spilling any that might drift into the ship's delicate electronic machinery. I don't think I'll even mention how we had to use the toilet.

***

A couple of days later, according to the chronometer, we were approximately one day from arrival, and Earth was gradually growing in the view from the shuttle windows.

Annemarie and I were drifting near the front window, just gazing out silently, and Ginna was nearby, staying close to Garek. None of us wanted to talk about what lay ahead.

Then suddenly, out of the corner of my eye, I caught sight of Darroch reaching into his suit through a small semi-sealed pocket. I knew what he usually carried under his left arm.

"Look out, he has a gun," I cried to Laken, before he could pull it out. Laken reacted like lightning, shoving Darroch back toward the airlock, but Darroch managed to hang onto the gun, and pointed it at Laken's head.

"So, you *are* the traitor! Have you been spying on me all these years, Darroch? You brought Celestia and her friends to me as a trap, didn't you? You knew I wouldn't be able to resist trying to cross the GAP."

"I only do my duty—to my true leaders—the Elders."

"The Morotani! But they're not true followers of the King, are they?"

"You might be surprised," Darroch said through gritted teeth. "You all are missing the Great Truth of the Chosen. We aren't meant to be puppets and servants to any king. We're meant to *each* be kings, with planets of our own to rule in the next life."

"That's always been the Morotani heresy," cried Laken. He tried reaching for the gun again, but Darroch kept it aimed at him.

"The Morotani have much more influence than any-one knows," Darroch hissed. "Once our great Temple in

Jerusalem is built, then all will know who's really true, and who's false."

"What does he mean, Mom?" I heard Annemarie ask.

Ginna shook her head. "I've felt all along something was wrong about this Temple."

"So, is Mauren in this with you?" Laken demanded then.

"Oh, you'd be surprised how many Morotani Elders are hidden in high places," sneered Darroch.

As he said this, he must have relaxed his grip just slightly on the gun's handle, for it drifted from his hand. I saw Garek grab it and sighed with relief.

But Darroch quickly unsealed the airlock and pulled the two men in with him. I tried to re-open the door, but the pilot stopped me.

"Don't open that, or we'll be sucked out into space if the outer door opens," he snapped. I could tell his real goal was to keep us from taking the ship, and that he didn't really care what happened to the three in the airlock.

"But our friends!" cried Annemarie.

"Garek!" Ginna screamed.

There was nothing we could do but watch the closed door, and hear the groans and scuffling coming over the com-system. Then there came a gunshot and a loud cry, followed by silence. My heart seemed to sink into my boots, and I saw Ginna put her face in her hands. Had she lost another loved one, like all the others she'd told me about?

Then the door slid open again, and Laken tumbled in, followed closely by Garek. Quickly they pulled the airlock closed behind them.

"What happened?" I cried and threw my arms around Laken. The motion sent us both spinning briefly, until we bumped a wall and drifted back toward the others.

At that moment, the assistant-pilot pointed his pistol at us. "No one make a move toward the controls, or you'll die."

"We almost had him," Laken was saying, at the same time. "But just as we were about to bind him, he grabbed the pistol from me and fired it. The hole in the hull broke the airlock's seal. We had to hold on to keep from being sucked out. Had barely enough time to get back in here. But apparently, Darroch let himself float out into space. He had a suit, but it will only keep him alive for a few hours."

"Why would he do something like that?" Annemarie asked. "Surely he knew it was suicide."

"I'm not sure," sighed Laken. "His com was breaking up, but I think he said something about no one keeping him from his destiny. Maybe he's totally convinced he'll have a planet of his own to rule in the next world."

"Will he find his planet out there?" Ginna wondered.

"He won't survive long enough in that suit to get to any planet," said Garek.

I could see how deeply they all felt betrayed, especially Laken. But all I felt was relief that Darroch was gone.

During all of this, the pilot was busy making calculations for our re-entry to Earth, while his partner kept his gun on us.

"Did you have something to do with this?" Laken demanded, turning to the pilot.

The man gave no answer, but asked, "Where is the gun now?"

"It must have been sucked out with Darroch," shrugged Garek.

"Well, get back into your seats," his assistant said tensely. "Re-entry begins in two minutes." Then he pulled on his helmet in silence.

All we could do was obey. Nothing had really changed, except that Darroch was gone. Even though I wasn't fond of him, I cringed to think what it must be like drifting out there alone. Knowing he was eventually going to die, and not being able to do anything about it. I hoped his beliefs—whatever they were—would help him to bear it.

CHAPTER 20
THROUGH THE DESERT

As soon as we exited the ship and removed our space-suits, guards re-tied our arms behind us. We were herded into a large hovercraft and zipped over the streets of Jerusalem. The next thing I knew, we were dropping into the huge courtyard of an ancient fortress.

"The Citadel," I heard Laken moan to himself.

Then they must have put some kind of sleeping gas into our vehicle, for when I woke, I was lying on a cold stone floor.

Slowly I opened my eyes and scanned the faces of my cell-mates. Ginna's eyes were closed, and she was leaning on Garek's shoulder. Annemarie was alone, leaning against the stone wall and staring at the floor of our cell.

"Annemarie?"

She looked up at me and I could see she, too, had been crying. "Well, what now, Celestia?"

"I have no idea," I sighed. "None of this makes sense.

Why would the MEI arrest us if they knew we were Believers? Is this all some kind of farce, and this king isn't really the True Lord, after all? Darroch and Laken seemed to be so sincere in their faith—uh, well, Laken, anyway. I don't understand any of this stuff about the Morotani."

She shrugged. "They had all the right words to say—especially Darroch—but there were times when I wondered if their actions were consistent with what they claimed to believe."

"Like what happened when we went clubbing in Toronto?"

"Yeah. That didn't seem to fit at all, did it?"

"Celestia, I'm so sorry I convinced you to go along with Laken's plans."

"Please, don't start, Annemarie. There's no point in regretting what we can't change."

"But I'm such a failure as a Believer, and I had high hopes of being cleansed by the Fountain in the Desert. It seems like it doesn't even exist. We've seen lots of deserts, but no fountains," she sighed.

"It does exist in the future," came Ginna's voice just then. "I experienced it myself—even though I was 'within' Martina. And I want this for you so badly, Annemarie, and for Garek, too. I know it will help us, if we can ever get to the right place and time."

"If the Lord is really here, why doesn't he help us?" I sighed.

"I was taught the Lord helps those who help themselves."

We all turned in surprise at the sound of Laken's voice.

"And you thought you'd help *yourself* to some fame and fortune—at our expense," Garek's voice said angrily.

"Go ahead and beat me up if you think it will help," muttered Laken. "You're right, I shouldn't have done it. I'm the one who deserves to spend the rest of my miserable life in this dungeon—not you."

I moved closer to the dark corner where I'd heard the sound of his voice. Was there a tone of repentance in it?

"Laken," I murmured and put my arms around him. "You aren't deceptive and evil like Darroch was. We knew what you were doing, and we hoped it would help us, too. But God is the one who helps us when we *can't* help our-selves—he forgives us for Kristos' sake. So, I just want you to know I—I forgive you."

He'd turned his face away from me at first, but my words startled him enough that he looked into my eyes. "Now I know you really *are* a true Believer, for only a per-son who's experienced the Lord's forgiveness can forgive like you just did, Celestia." His voice began to quaver.

I pulled him closer to me, cradling his head against my chest, feeling sobs racking his body. There wasn't a sound around us. Everyone else was apparently speechless.

At last, Laken's crying subsided, and I was able to bring him over to where the others were. We all sat in a circle, holding hands.

It was the kind of circle we made to cross the GAP when we fled Tacoma. Or even before, when we'd first tried to cross to the Fountain in the Desert. Yet I knew we didn't have enough power to get out of this Time Well. Then I realized this circle also reminded me of when I prayed with my family, but I couldn't find any words to say, until Ginna started whispering:

"Our Father, who art in heaven—"

"Hallowed be thy name," Annemarie's voice joined in.

Then I heard Laken. "Thy kingdom come, thy will be done."

"On earth as it is in heaven," came Ginna's voice again.

I'd never heard this prayer before but could tell by the ancient language that it must be from The Book.

"Give us this day our daily bread," Laken continued. "And forgive us our trespasses."

"As we forgive those who trespass against us," came Garek's voice suddenly.

'Where did they all learn this?' I asked myself.

"And lead us not into temptation," Ginna whispered.

"But deliver us from evil." Annemarie took a deep breath, as she said this. "For thine is the kingdom, and the power, and the glory, forever."

Then came a long silence at the end of the prayer, and so I added, "Amen."

"We call this 'The Lord's Prayer'," Ginna said. "The Book says when his disciples asked him how to pray, this is what he told them."

Gradually the heaviness of fear and sorrow lifted off my shoulders. What was different now? We were still locked in this cold, damp, and dark place. But now we realized we had each other and could be stronger together than we were apart.

"I feel sorry for Darroch," whispered Laken. "He'll never know this need I feel, this great desire I have to serve and help my friends."

"He just wanted to be a king himself," I added.

"You know," Ginna sighed. "That's what Martina, Jael, and Jon found on every planet they visited—the sin of humans trying to be gods, lords of themselves and everything around them. It was the underlying problem everywhere—whether the System, the Pyrrhians, the Nosticenes—anyone."

"And now we've seen it here on Earth, too," murmured Annemarie.

"It's the original sin, you know," I said. "When the serpent convinced Eve in the Garden of Eden to eat the forbidden fruit, that's exactly what he said:

" 'When you eat this fruit,' he told her, 'You will not surely die. For God knows that when you eat of it your eyes will be opened, and you will be like God, knowing good and evil'."

"Knowing good and evil doesn't sound like such a bad thing. I'm confused again," said Garek.

"The problem is Adam and Eve were made in God's

image—and since God is wholly good, they were meant to know only good. But when the serpent—who was Satan in disguise—tricked them into thinking they could be their own gods, then evil came into the world."

"Celestia, you know so much about The Book. I wish I could read it more."

"Perhaps you'll still get the chance, Garek," Laken said, moving closer to me and putting his arm across my shoulders. Now, somehow, I felt no fear of him.

"I remember a verse my mother taught me," I added. "It's from a book called *Psalms*."

"That means 'songs', in ancient Hebrew," Ginna nodded. "How did it go?"

"I'll try to remember as much as I can—it's helped me in times of trouble, so perhaps it can help you, too. It's *Psalm Forty-six:*

" 'God is our refuge and strength, an ever-present help in trouble. Therefore, we will not fear, though the earth gives way and the mountains fall into the heart of the sea'—"

"That sounds like what happened in the earthquake we went through."

"Yes, Annemarie, it sure does. Here's more of what I remember, 'There is a river whose streams make glad the city of God'."

"We saw that river with Eli, after the Fountain in the Desert," Ginna cried, "And tasted it, too—nothing else I ever drink will taste so good."

"My mom said that, too," I nodded. "I don't remember all the rest of the Psalm, but I know it also says, 'God is within her, and she will not fall; God will help her at the break of day'."

"Do you think God will help *us* at the break of day?" asked Garek. It hurt to hear the doubt and pain in his voice.

"We can't even tell if it's day or night down here," sighed Annemarie.

"I guess I was hoping the new City of God would already be here, when you told us the True King was reigning." Ginna turned to Laken as she said this.

"I have no answer for you," he sighed. "At first things were improving—much better than they were during the War of Unification."

"I've heard a verse," I said, "in the book of *Isaiah*, where God says, 'As the heavens are higher than the earth, so are my ways higher than your ways and my thoughts than your thoughts'."

"You're right," said Ginna. "God can see things that we have no inkling of."

"Sometimes we think we know how the Lord will work, but he has a totally different idea," I murmured.

"Right, Celestia—we're just like little specks here on one tiny planet in all the vastness of the Universe," Laken added.

"What can we possibly do to please a Lord that powerful?" asked Annemarie.

"Nothing," I sighed. "Nothing but stand in awe of him." After another long silence, as we each tried to wrap our minds around these thoughts, I heard Ginna begin to sing softly:

> *O Lord, how shall I meet you, how welcome you aright?*
> *Your people long to greet you, my hope, my heart's*
>   *delight!*
> *O kindle, Lord most holy, your lamp within my breast*
> *To do in spirit lowly all that may please you best.*
>
> *I lay in fetters groaning; you came to set me free.*
> *I stood my shame bemoaning; you came to honor me.*
> *A glorious crown you gave me, a treasure safe on high*
> *That will not fail or leave me, as earthly riches fly.*

"Boy, Ginna, that song really sums up where we find ourselves here in prison."

"Songs come to me often, Celestia. It especially happened when we were in the desert with Eli."

"I still wish we could find the Fountain," sighed Annemarie.

"If the Lord means us to, we will—in his time," I whispered.

"You know what this reminds me of?" said Ginna.

"What?"

"The story of when Paul and Silas were chained in prison and began singing hymns of praise to the Lord."

"Then an earthquake came and their chains fell off—freeing them," I smiled back at her.

"Guess we need another earthquake," said Garek.

Suddenly, we heard the clinking sound of keys, and the door of our cell slowly swung open. We expected to see a guard, but instead there was someone dressed all in white. In fact, his clothes were so bright they gleamed.

"Are you an angel?" I heard Ginna asking in awe.

"Come with me," was all he said, in a voice reverberating with power.

The five of us stood and began to follow the shining form down the corridor past other cells, and then we were taken into a square room with windows that had no bars.

"Wait here," he said, and seemed to disappear in an instant, leaving the door open.

"Now I feel like Saint Peter in *Acts*," I whispered.

"What?" Garek sounded confused.

"He was one of the Lord's disciples who was imprisoned, and an angel led him out of the jail."

"I remember hearing that story, too," added Ginna.

I smiled at them, thankful I'd taken time to read The Book my father kept hidden in our cave. Somehow, I sensed in my heart something good was about to happen.

Suddenly, there came a sound of footsteps, and the door to the room clicked closed. I looked up expecting to see another guard, come to take us back to our cell. But surprise and a strange thrill filled me instead.

A tall man stood there, dressed in white robes trimmed in gold. On his head was a simple band of gold encircling his dark brown hair, which framed a bronzed face. From the band dangled a golden cross, resting in the middle of his forehead. There wasn't a blinding light, like the angel shone with. But there was some kind of aura around him that took my breath away. And his eyes were like nothing I'd ever seen before—a deep golden brown. In them was a look of love, combined with great sorrow. I felt as though he could see into my soul—to every thought and action I'd ever done—both the good and the bad. I sank to my knees, and my companions did the same.

"My Lord, and my God," I murmured.

Then his face broke into the most beautiful smile I'd ever seen, sending warmth into my very soul. There was no doubt in my mind. I was in the presence of the True King, the one my parents talked about so much.

By now I was bowing low, my forehead nearly touching the floor—it seemed the only proper thing to do. Nearby, I could hear sobs and Annemarie's voice:

"Oh, Lord, please forgive me. I've been so blind. I do believe—please help my unbelief."

"Yes," I heard my own voice echo. "I keep doubting you and wondering if you care, if you really know what you're doing. What a foolish creature I've been."

Suddenly, I knew I was no better than these others I'd been trying to guide to the Fountain. But then I felt his hand on my shoulder and heard him whisper, "You are still my faithful servant."

Laken was lying prostrate on the floor, beginning to sob again. "I've been extremely selfish—using others for my own personal gain."

There was no sound at all from Garek.

"My dear children," came a rich and sonorous voice. "I've loved you since the foundation of the world. You have no need to fear, for I've made the payment demanded for all your mistakes. First, my dear Celestia…"

I felt a strong, warm touch on my head, and then he took my hand and pulled me up. All at once I was enfolded in an embrace reminding me of my father hugging me as a child. But this one was sending strength and hope into my very soul. I knew beyond a doubt how much I was loved.

"You even know my name," I breathed, not daring to look up.

"I have called you each by name." I could hear the smiling warmth in his voice. "Celestia, Ginna, Annemarie, Garek, and even you, Laken."

"Do you know *everyone's* names?" I couldn't keep the wonder out of my voice.

He lifted my chin so I could see the glow in his eyes as he answered, "Oh yes, I know them all—the millions, billions, and even trillions."

My mind was reeling, trying to grasp an intelligence so vast. There were no words to describe it. Then I saw the scars in his hands.

Soon, all of us were standing in a circle around him, gazing from him to each other, totally speechless. Then he seated us on the floor and sat down to join us.

"This reminds me of the story of Mary sitting at your feet," whispered Ginna.

He smiled more broadly. "Ah yes, my friends Mary and Martha, who helped make my first earthly sojourn so much more pleasant. Friendship is important to everyone."

"You really are Kristos, aren't you?" came Garek's voice. "The same Lord my mother called 'Yeshua'?"

"Yes, I am he."

"And you really died on that cross?" I asked.

He nodded. "Like the phoenix coming from the ashes, I arose from the fires of death."

We sat in silence for what seemed a long time—it was like sitting in the sunshine on a summer day, with no need to move, or speak, or do anything but soak in the warmth. At last though, I had to ask my question:

"Lord, if you *are* King here and now, why are there still prisons, and guards, and betrayals? Why are we here?"

"Ah—well, as you've guessed already, my kingdom is not a worldly one. What is happening now is a test of humankind's true nature. There is no Devil to blame anything on, for he's been sent to the Abyss. The trials of the wars just past were very hard, but now comes a test perhaps even more difficult to pass—the test of peace and prosperity.

"Many times, it's been the peace after the war where most have stumbled and fallen. My people never understood the first time I came—that the Kingdom of God is within—even though I told them many times. Two Millennia have passed, each one teaching another lesson to humankind. In this next one, they will see what their hearts truly hold. So now, they'll have the earthly king they desired, and they'll learn what this does—and does not—give them."

"And at the end of this Millennium?" I whispered.

"You've read it in my Book. The final judgment will come at the end of time."

"What about Laken?" asked Annemarie, with a fearful look in her eyes.

He glanced toward Laken and smiled. "I think he's seen his error, and now knows what true forgiveness means."

"Thanks to Celestia."

This time when Laken smiled at me, I found myself beginning to think of him as a friend.

"Thank you, Lord, for giving me time to change my ways," said Garek suddenly.

"For-giving is what I'm all about now," said the deep voice. "The judgment is reserved for the End of the Age."

"When will it come?" asked Ginna.

"No one knows the day or the hour—not even me. Only my Father knows."

"Lord," said Annemarie, "We really wanted—and needed—to find your cleansing Fountain. Can you help us?"

"You've already found it, my child."

"How?"

"I am the living water, you see. Yes, the Fountain in the Desert will appear in its time, for those who have need of it. But I've already given you the forgiveness you seek. You just need to receive it—the way a child receives a gift."

Ginna was smiling now, her face radiant. Her daughter's face was shining, too, but covered with tears. Garek and Laken were even wiping at their eyes.

I felt a strong touch wipe the last of my tears, and then I saw him touch his own cheek with the dampness. He did the same to the others, too. "Please remember," he whispered, "That for tears like these, I died. The price has been paid for all time."

Then he cupped his hands, and water appeared in them as if from nowhere. He held his hands over my head, and water dripped through my hair. Next, I felt him make a cross sign on my forehead, a wet version of the gold one he wore.

When he'd done this to the others, he said, "Your human failings have been put to death with me. Now rise with me into new life in the Spirit."

"What should we do now, Lord?" I asked.

"The same thing I've always told my disciples: 'What I say to you, I say to everyone: "Watch!" For you do not know the day or the hour when the Son of Man will return. At that time, if anyone says to you, "Look, here is the Christ!" or, "There he is!" do not believe it. For false Christs and false prophets will appear and perform great signs and miracles to deceive even the elect—if that were possible. See, I have told you ahead of time.'

"And now, my children, you must go back to the time where you each are most needed."

He stood and joined our hands with his in a circle. The floor fell away from my feet, and I knew I was somewhere in a GAP.

***

The next thing I knew, I was standing in a grassy clearing, near the edge of a dense forest. Someone was holding tightly to my left hand. Turning, I saw Laken gazing at me in wonder.

To one side of us was a cluster of huts, where I heard the shouts of young children. In front of me was a green hillside, and when I looked up, I saw my mother and Daiah running toward me, calling my name.

CHAPTER 21
THE TRUE FOUNTAIN

Ginna opened her eyes and found herself standing in her own front yard. The little house on the edge of Deer Path, Colorado hadn't changed at all. The porch still sagged in the middle, and the steps were rotting along the edges. Some shingles were missing on the roof, and the tall trees hanging over the house still needed to be trimmed before their branches fell onto the house in some storm.

She felt her heart sinking. 'So, *this* was where the Lord wanted me? Back here in the place I least wanted to be all my life?'

But then she felt a warm hand holding hers.

"Ginna?" came Garek's voice. "Is this your house?"

Speechless, she nodded.

"Well, it looks like the King has sent us both to your time," he smiled. Then he gathered her into his arms and kissed her.

Ginna felt tears overflowing from her eyes, but now they were tears of joy. "Welcome to Colorado, Garek. I hope you'll be all right here."

"I've already told you—whenever and wherever you are—that's where I want to be. But I do wonder what century he's sent us to."

Ginna glanced around the yard and saw it looked like a typical winter day. Could they really have come back to the very day she'd left? Then she saw the light blue car sitting in the gravel driveway.

"I'd say it's the Twenty-first Century, and it looks like I have to return Annemarie's rental car for her."

He laughed explosively. "I'd love to drive to Denver. But how will we get back?"

"We'll have to take my old clunker, too," she smiled. "I'd better drive that one—it's temperamental."

"No problem," he squeezed her hand gently.

"I hope you'll find something to do here—and won't be bored with this simple little place."

"If you have any books, that will be great."

"Yes, I have lots of them," she smiled.

"Then, I'm sure I'll keep occupied," he chuckled.

"Maybe we can go see Yellowstone—while it still exists," she said.

"Sure!" he laughed. "What a great idea. And we need to arrange for that wedding ceremony in Salt Lake City— to reaffirm the vows we made in Toronto."

She nodded, then sighed. "That was in the *future*, too. This is getting so confusing. I wonder if there will be any more GAP-crossing for us, now that we've personally met the True First-born."

He smiled down at her and kissed the top of her head. "I think we should leave that up to Him and concentrate on where we are now. For starters, I can do some repairs on your house."

With that, he lifted her into his arms, carried her up the steps, and through the front door.

"Once we're officially married in this time, it will be your house too," she smiled into his blue eyes.

***

The first thing Annemarie felt was snow on her arms and head, and she shivered. For an instant a red shape seemed to hover above her, and a voice filled her mind: "I will never leave you or forsake you."

Trying to get her eyes to focus through the swirling flakes, she saw she was standing on a street corner. Tall skyscrapers loomed in the distance, and in front of her a rectangle of light shone on the sidewalk.

From the shape of some of the buildings, she thought perhaps she was in Denver—but in which century? The buildings didn't look very futuristic, but now she knew this wasn't always a good clue.

The building in front of her was made of brick and looked very old. Looking upward toward the sky, she saw it had a pointed tower and realized with a shock it was a steeple. She was standing in front of an old church. A faint sound of music came to her ears from the windows.

Slowly she climbed the snow-covered steps and pushed at the door, not really expecting it to open. But it did, with a slight creaking sound.

Inside, the room was dimly lit by one lamp near the front of the sanctuary. The familiar rows of wooden pews were empty. The sounds she heard were coming from an upright piano far ahead of her. A voice was singing a familiar tune, but she couldn't make out all the words until she got to the front few rows:

Bright morning star, true living vine,
Builder of mountains and keeper of time.
Author of life, you flow through my veins.
Give me your breath and I will run in your strength.

Oh Jesus, give me strength for the race,
Turn my back on the past and reach for your face.
I call out to you, for your promise is true:
Oh Jesus, give me strength for the race.

"Strength for the Race" Copyright 2005, by Gregory A. DeMuth/Sacred Ground Music. Used by permission.

Something about the music drew her toward it. Even though her feet didn't want to walk up there, she found herself powerless to stop. The piano was turned at an angle, so she couldn't see who was playing, but now she could tell the voice was male.

"That song really says it all," she heard her own voice saying. "The Lord is truly the keeper of time—he's taken me to many times and places. I've seen the works of his hands in the most amazing ways, the stars and the mountains, and how he gives his people strength in the most terrible circumstances. I've seen how he comes to the rescue of those who need him most, even though they've done nothing to deserve it."

Suddenly, all the things happening to her in the past few years—in three different centuries—seemed to fall off her shoulders. She mentally laid them all at the foot of the cross standing beside the altar. Tears were streaming down her cheeks, but this time they were tears of joy. Kneeling at the foot of that cross, she finally knew the Lord had forgiven her and would always be there for her.

"Now I know what true love is—it's forgiveness. I saw Celestia forgive Laken, and Ginna forgive Garek. And now I know God has forgiven me."

There was a slight shuffling sound to her right, and she realized the music had stopped. Without looking up, she sensed a young man standing there. Did she hear a sob?

"Annemarie? Is it really you?"

The sound of his voice cut right into her soul—this was impossible—unless the King was the one who'd done it. "David?"

She felt him take her hand, drawing her to stand beside him. "What are you doing here?"

"The Lord of Heaven and Earth sent me. I need to tell you how sorry I am—how wrong I was. I don't expect you to love me anymore, after all I did to you, but will you please forgive me? David, I've never been able to stop loving you."

He just looked at her in silence.

"I know you don't believe any of this," she continued. "I barely can myself. I was about to jump from a hotel window tonight—right here in Denver. And someone came to stop me, a young woman from the future."

"Was she an angel?"

"I guess you could say that."

Now he sat down in the front pew, shaking his head. "I've had this dream over and over—that you come like this. But I thought it was only wishful thinking. It seemed impossible."

"But didn't the Lord once say 'with God all things are possible'?"

He nodded slowly and raised his head to look into her eyes. "Are you real? Or just an illusion of my mind?"

She reached her hand toward him, afraid of what he might do, but he grabbed it, and pulled her to him.

"Praise God! You *are* real!" he cried.

Outside, the snow continued to fall, and there in the front of the church their tears fell, but they were not all tears of regret.

PREVIEW OF
THE PEAKS SAGA, BOOK 6

"BEYOND THE WORLD"

PROLOGUE
IMAGES

There was nothing but darkness before his eyes as he moved slowly through the trees. Somehow, he could sense them and avoid walking into their rough-barked trunks. Perhaps it was the way the ground level changed as his hooves neared their roots.

He tossed his head, shaking out his tangled mane and nickered softly. Then he pushed air from his nostrils in a loud *whoosh*.

Lowering his head, he chomped off a few blades of grass. It was still too early in the spring for very many of the new fresh blades, so he had to settle for the dried remains of last year's crop. It wasn't too bad, though—it tasted like the straw his master had fed him—back when he still had a home.

That was now a hazy faded memory, though. He couldn't really measure the time, but there had been numerous periods of light and darkness. The weather had gone through its full sequence—from the chill of the snowy time through the greening up and the hot days of long sunlight—and then back to the long darkness and the fading of fresh and green things—into the cold, and back out again.

These cycles had always been a part of his life, but before, there was some shelter provided for him from the wet rain and the cold snow. Now he had to find his own shelter—sometimes in a rocky overhang, or under some of the taller, thicker trees. The cycles passed over him, and he just took what each day brought. Numbering the passage of seasons was not part of his nature. His only awarenesses were the immediate needs—food, water, and shelter.

This night, there were no lights—he didn't know to call them stars or moon. Neither did he know to call the dark concealing these things clouds. All he knew was his sense of sight had little use at the moment. He was using his keen hearing and sense of smell, along with the touch of his hooves on the ground, and occasionally the brush of his flanks or legs against some low vegetation.

Suddenly his eyes did see something—two yellow lights glowing between the trees ahead of him. Stepping closer, he saw the eyes of some animal. It was lower to the ground than he, and emitted a low growl. At first, he snorted in fear, but when the eyes didn't move any closer, he sniffed more deeply. There was no smell of threat. In fact, there was a smell he hadn't known for a very long time.

Moving closer still, he could now see this was not a wolf but a big black dog with pointed ears. It gave a whining sound and stepped closer to him. Now he knew this scent—it came from humans.

The dog brushed gently against his foreleg and gave a short bark. Then it started off through the trees to his right. Without any hesitation, he followed.

***

Dark and cold and damp. These were the only things the man was aware of. For awhile he'd shivered—his body trying to generate some warmth by movement of his muscles. That hadn't been enough, as the cold settled into his bones. Now there was probably no way to dislodge it.

Sometimes—perhaps in another lifetime—his eyes had seen light. There were faces, too—a young woman who looked vaguely familiar—looming from somewhere deep in his memory. Had she been special to him? Did he know her name?

He shook his head—the effort felt like trying to move a huge and heavy weight. No—there were no memories now. His mind was as cold, dark, and empty as the place where he lay.

***

Stars were falling, streaking across the black of the night sky, pieces of an asteroid that began to break up as it entered the planet's atmosphere.

No human eyes beheld the sight, but in a golden sky a large hawk-like bird circled, riding the thermals.

They were nothing more than particles following their appointed rounds in space—a cosmos that is mostly empty, within and without. What was keeping it from collapsing into chaos?

***

It felt so good to stretch his muscles after all the ages of confinement. A laugh rumbled deep inside him, and a sudden puff of smoke came from his nostrils. This made him laugh again with delight, and the smoke became a red-orange flame.

Ah, yes, this was his favorite form! All too often he had to disguise his true identity—posing perhaps as a handsome human male with sleek dark hair—sometimes as a threatening animal, such as a wolf. The form he most detested, though, was when he had to imitate the golden glowing body of an angel, one of the Enemy's trusted servants.

This memory sent waves of rage through him, and bright blue flames shot from his mouth and nostrils. He'd been one of them once—many eons ago—but now was cast out. No matter how he tried to reassume his original form, it never quite fit anymore. In fact, the very thought of it made him itch with an irritation that only got worse the more he scratched it with his long, curving claws.

In anger he spread his huge leathery wings, admiring the dark shadows they cast across the landscape below where he sat, perched on the edge of a craggy cliff. At least now he was free of the chains that had bound him for so long.

'The Enemy thinks he has only released me for a time,' he hissed to himself. 'But he underestimates me. I still have powers he hasn't seen, and when I unleash them…'

The deep chuckling in his throat emerged as a roar. This ominous sound echoed off the mountains all around, as he launched his huge serpentine form into space and took flight.

THANK YOU

Thank you for joining me. If you liked the story and have a minute to spare, I would appreciate a short comment on the page or site where you bought the book.

Reviews from readers like you make a huge difference to helping new readers find stories similar to The Peaks series: *The Fountain and the Desert.*

- Amazon
- Barnes & Noble
- Goodreads
- iBooks

Thank you!

M. F. Erler

ABOUT THE AUTHOR

M.F. (Mary Frances) Erler is a music teacher, outdoor educator, and author of fantasy fiction and non-fiction. Her teaching career has spanned over 25 years, and she has been writing most of her life. Her first Christian-based science-fiction book, "The Peaks at the Edge of the World" has been re-written and revised in 2017.

Erler has been writing most of her life. In fact, some of the characters in *The Peaks Saga* were initially conceived in her youth. Her lifelong goal has been to bring spiritual ideas into fantasy-fiction, in the spirit of writers like J.R.R. Tolkien and C.S. Lewis. She enjoys public speaking and sharing her faith journey. She is an approved speaker for Women's Connections, a Stonecroft Ministry.

Now that she has finished ***The Peaks Saga***, she is embarking on a new venture in historical fiction, where her modern-day characters time-travel back into the lives of their ancestors. So, in the future, watch for more tales in *Journeys Beyond the Peaks.*

Her books are designed to appeal to young adults and all who are young at heart. Among her many hobbies, Erler especially enjoys travel. She has been to several countries, including China, New Zealand, the British Isles, and Western Europe, as well as Canada, Mexico, Jamaica, and 43 of the 50 States. Her favorite mode of travel is cruising, but her current favorite place is her home in Montana.

Along with fantasy, true science, and science fiction, she is also a student of history, comparative religion, ecology, and music. Previous publications include non-fiction articles in *Today's Christian Parent,* and *Social Studies and the Young Learner,* as well as poems and short sketches in Standard Publishing Program Books. In addition, she has produced *Music in God's World,* a music curriculum for preschools, and *Wonders of Creation, an Environmental Education Curricula* for use in schools and camp settings. She has worked as a newspaper reporter and columnist, and was writer for various U.S. Forest Service Publications, including being in charge of producing the book, *Targhee Lodgepole-Tragedy or Opportunity?*

She has a Bachelor of Science in Environmental Education and Biology from Colorado State University, and a Masters of Music Education from Concordia University-Chicago. In her senior year of high school, she was awarded a prize for her writing by the National Council of Teachers of English, the Quill and Scroll Award for Journalism, and a National Merit Scholarship.

Her love of singing has led to participation in many choirs and Acapella groups, which enabled her to perform at two International Sweet Adelines conventions in Nashville and Houston. She sang with these women's barbershop groups for 18 years. Hobbies include reading, singing, playing several musical instruments, and teaching piano and guitar lessons. She and her husband have two adult children. All make their home in the northwest.

Connect with Frances at:
mferler@peaksandbeyond.com
Or follow her blog at PeaksAndBeyond.com
(MFErler.blogspot.com)

www.ingramcontent.com/pod-product-compliance
Lightning Source LLC
Chambersburg PA
CBHW070623170726
48291CB00003B/845